the Peonies

Summer in the City

The Peonies: Summer in the City is published under Emerge, a sectionalized division under Di Angelo Publications, Inc.

Emerge is an imprint of Di Angelo Publications.

Printed in the United States of America.

Di Angelo Publications
4265 San Felipe #1100
Houston, Texas 77027

Library of Congress
The Peonies: Summer in the City
ISBN: 978-1-955690-30-0

Words: Alix Sloan & Jennie Willink
Cover Design: Savina Deianova
Interior Design: Kimberly James
Cover & Interior Illustrations: Andrea Sutjipta
Editors: Ashley Crantas, Elizabeth Geeslin Zinn, Willy Rowberry, Theresa Silvester

Downloadable via Kindle, iBooks, NOOK, and Google Play.

1. Juvenile Fiction --- Social Themes --- Friendship
2. Juvenile Fiction --- Family --- Alternative Family
3. Juvenile Fiction --- Lifestyles --- City & Town Life

the Peonies

Summer in the City

Alix Sloan and Jennie Willink

For all of the inspiring girls in our lives, and
for our own New York friend-family.
We love you.

Contents

CHAPTER ONE

the Big Bomb

Anyone could see how excited they were.

Esme practically skipped along the route home from school, leaping over the bigger sidewalk cracks like a preteen gazelle.

"Wait up!" Poppy pleaded. Saddled with shorter legs than her exuberant friend, she lengthened her stride to try to keep pace.

It's not that the girls disliked school—they had even stayed late to say goodbye to their friends and teachers! It's just that they were *so* excited for summer, and Esme couldn't wait to get it started.

There were about a million things for two eleven-year-old girls to do in New York City: swim at the community pool, visit their favorite park, bike along the river, peruse all of the shops in the neighborhood, hang out at Poppy's dad's photo studio, plus all of the new adventures they planned to cook up. Today they'd learned that Chelsea

Piers was offering a day of free trapeze lessons for kids.

"Do you think they'll ever let us go to the Piers by ourselves?" Poppy asked, finally catching up to Esme when she stopped at a red light.

The girls were allowed to walk to and from school alone and within three blocks of their apartment building. But that was it, and that was only because all of the neighbors knew and looked out for them.

"It's just across town and we're practically in middle school," Esme reasoned. "It can't hurt to ask."

Poppy was doubtful. But if anyone could convince their parents to loosen the reins, it was Esme. She had a natural gift for negotiation.

The girls approached Mr. and Mrs. Wu's Parkside Bodega, which felt like the official start of their neighborhood. Like all of the other bodegas or small shops you find every few blocks in New York City, it was full of grocery staples like milk and eggs, fresh vegetables and flowers, emergency batteries and aspirin, and a deli counter for sandwiches to go. It even had its very own black and gray striped bodega cat called Zipper. The shop had been in the neighborhood for years and was one of the very first places the girls were allowed to walk to alone.

As they got closer, Poppy and Esme saw Mrs. Wu out front spraying vegetables with water to keep them looking fresh. She was of indeterminate age, but definitely older than their parents. Beyond that, the girls couldn't have guessed. She also, as far as they knew, had no first name.

And they had no idea how she did it, but she always knew when someone was coming up behind her. She would shut off her sprayer, step aside, and greet each passerby.

"Hello Peonies," Mrs. Wu nodded.

Everywhere they went, it was Esme and Poppy, Poppy and Esme. Never one without the other, which is how they got their nickname. Neighbors started calling them "P" and "E"; then that got shortened to "P-n-E," which became the word "Peony," the beautiful spring flower. Eventually, everyone started calling them Peony or The Peonies. Nobody even remembers when it first started. But it stuck. And once Poppy's mom, Sasha, told the girls all about the intricate, fragrant blooms, they loved it.

"Hello, Mrs. Wu," the girls replied in unison as they passed by.

Sasha had taught the girls that peonies symbolized many things, including good fortune, honor, and compassion, which they knew were important qualities. And peonies came in practically a zillion shades of pink, which was, coincidentally, The Peonies' favorite color. They were even used as medicine in olden days, something Poppy particularly liked because she was pretty sure she wanted to be a veterinarian, or a doctor, when she grew up.

"Peonies are going to be out of season soon, right?" Esme asked as they continued.

"That's right. April through June." Poppy read constantly and had a great memory for random facts.

Up ahead, their neighbor Julie, who they'd also known

their whole lives, was standing in front of her shop, Lucky Stars. The little brick storefront sat wedged between the new coffee shop that used to be a bookstore, and the old barber shop, now a bike repair. Julie was tall with wild, wavy brown hair and caramel-colored eyes. She often wore colorful leather jackets with jeans in the winter and funky dresses in the summer. Today she was wearing an oversized, long-sleeved, pinstriped men's shirt cinched with a thick black belt. She usually wore motorcycle boots, and today was no exception. In the back corner of the store, at an elaborate workbench with tiny drawers for housing gems and supplies, Julie made beautiful custom jewelry. Lucky Stars sold her creations along with all sorts of other things like journals, cookbooks, candles, soaps, frames, and art. Everybody in the neighborhood shopped there. Julie was super nice, had great taste, and had a shop dog named Scribbles. If she knew you, she'd ring you up with a ten percent discount. Poppy's mom said this combination made her a shrewd businesswoman. The girls just thought of her as the cool big sister they both wished they had.

"Hello, ladies! Looking good today!"

The girls smiled. They'd taken extra care preparing their matching outfits for the last day of school—black and white polka dot t-shirts, hot pink leggings, and black high-top sneakers. But even though they were as close as twin sisters, occasionally dressed alike, and shared a nickname, The Peonies looked nothing alike. Poppy was small for her age with a dark complexion and curly tresses she almost always pulled back into a ponytail. She had a square jaw, perfectly proportioned button nose, and almond-shaped eyes. Small, strong, and agile, Poppy excelled at jujitsu. Esme, on the other hand, had long, blonde hair, deep-set hazel eyes, and pale skin that sunburned easily. Her oval face was dominated by a "regal" nose she hated; it just seemed too big to her, but her parents promised she'd grow into it. Her tall, slender frame was perfect for dance and lap swimming.

"And what are my pals The Peonies up to tonight?" Julie inquired.

"It's family dinner night, Julie." Poppy sounded exasperated.

"Wow, it's Friday already?" Julie sometimes forgot what day of the week it was, claiming that when you're self-employed, all the days blend together. "Well, I finished some new designs today if you have time for a visit."

Esme looked at Poppy hopefully for a moment. Then they both shook their heads. The girls loved hanging out at Lucky Stars and being the first to see Julie's new creations. But it was almost dinnertime, and they knew that the key to keeping the freedoms they'd been granted was to never, ever worry their parents by coming home late.

"Not tonight," Poppy answered.

The girls kept moving and they soon reached the corner of their block. Halfway down, among a row of apartment buildings, was the six-story brick building they'd lived in their entire lives. Esme lived on the top floor with her parents, Kay and Sam, and her older brother, Grady. Poppy and her mom Sasha were on the second floor.

Poppy admired their building as they approached the door. "Prettiest on the block!"

With faded green awnings, a white iron fire escape, and twenty white metal stars the size of dinner plates stuck to the façade, their building was distinctive. Prettiest on the block? Maybe not. But they certainly thought so.

"That's for sure," Esme agreed, her stomach growling loudly. She was always hungry and would eat practically anything.

"What do you think is for dinner?" Poppy giggled.

"I don't know. But I'm positively famished!" Esme answered, clutching her belly dramatically.

"I bet it'll be something special for the last day of school."

Poppy pulled an enormous gold key stamped with Do Not Duplicate out of her unicorn-printed backpack, reached up, and inserted it into their building's heavy metal and frosted glass front door. The girls pushed it open together and raced for the elevator.

As The Peonies stepped into the sixth-floor hallway, they noticed a strong burning smell.

"Ooooh..." Poppy stopped, wiggled her nose like a

bunny, and smiled. “You know what that means.”

“Pizza!” Esme answered. “This day couldn’t get any better!”

Every Friday since the girls were born, the two families had gotten together for family dinner. Sometimes it was at Poppy’s apartment, sometimes Esme’s. They kept it up even after Poppy’s parents split up. Her dad, Will, still joined them once in a while.

Part of the Friday night tradition was trying new recipes, and the deal was, if dinner turned out okay, no matter what was made, the kids had to at least try it. They’d eaten liver and onions (gross), lasagna soup (weird), and kale succotash (yum). But if the recipe went wrong or got too complicated for the grown-ups, they ordered pizza.

Esme pushed open the door to 6B and stepped from the stained brown carpet of the hallway onto the polished hardwood of the big open room that was their kitchen, eating, and living area.

A favorite framed photograph of the two families, posed together in a triangle like a human pyramid, hung on the wall just inside the apartment. Will had taken it a few years ago when he and Sasha were still together. The other three parents were kneeling on the bottom row. Kay and Sam were somehow kissing while supporting the kids on their backs. Sasha smiled broadly, probably at Will behind the camera. Esme and Grady balanced on the second row with their skinny sibling arms intertwined. And, of course, Poppy, the peanut, teetered on top.

"Happy last day of school, girls!" Sam called from the kitchen. Wearing oven mitts and an apron, Esme's dad stood over the kitchen sink, holding a large smoking pot. His red hair stuck up all sweaty and gross, and he had a familiar look of frustration on his face.

"What did you ruin this time, Dad?" Esme teased.

"Don't be mean, Esmeralda," Kay scolded. "You know how much your dad likes to cook."

Like their daughters, Kay and Sasha couldn't have been more different. And they were also great friends. They met in college and had been close ever since. Kay even introduced Sasha to Will, a cute and talented photographer she abd Sam met in Art History class.

Kay was as blonde as her daughter Esme and favored comfortable, flowy clothing, loose painters' smocks, and colorful scarves, and she left the scent of jasmine oil behind wherever she went. Because Sasha was a lawyer, she had to dress up for work. But she always added a cool vintage flair, like a silk flower or rhinestone pin, to her boring suits. She wore her black hair in a chic style, cropped close to her head.

The two moms stood at an open window, fanning out the smoky air. Sasha teetered on four-inch heels, flapping a magazine with one hand while trying to keep Kay's turquoise scarf out of her mouth with the other. Kay's billowy white sleeves made her look like a giant moth. The whole scene was ridiculous.

"I was trying to make fondue." Sam gestured to a

baguette and vegetables he'd prepped for dipping. "But I got so busy chopping I forgot to watch the cheese."

"The pizza is already ordered," Sasha added, kicking off her heels and flopping her petite frame down on the deep blue couch. "And we are not waiting for Grady."

"Yay!" Poppy exclaimed. "Do we have time for a game of UNO?" She loved UNO and was on a six-week Friday night winning streak.

"After you help Sam turn those veggies into a salad," Sasha agreed, giving Poppy's puff of a ponytail a playful tug.

"And we need to make our drinks," Esme added.

The first thing The Peonies did every family dinner night was make a mystery soda mixture—one-half whatever juice was in the refrigerator, sometimes a mixture of two, and one-half bubbly water. They usually put a slice or two of fruit in also. They loved making different flavor combinations. Last week it was cranberry mango with lime. They raced to the kitchen to explore ingredients for tonight's creation.

Two large pizzas and three games of UNO later, the girls cleared the table while finishing off the last of their pomegranate orange sodas. They were about to head into Esme's bedroom to plan their summer when Poppy's mom stopped them.

"Girls. Come. Sit down." Sasha went to her favorite spot on the couch and patted the cushion next to her. Sam sat in the big, worn-out leather chair. Kay stood, looking out the window and twisting the wedding ring on her finger—something she did only when she was stressed out.

The girls exchanged puzzled looks and joined the group. Was someone sick?

"Esme," Sam said, "you know how we've been talking about seeing more of Grandma Martha?"

"Sure. Is she coming to visit?"

Grandma Martha was Sam's mother. She lived in California, where he grew up.

"Not exactly."

"We don't have to go there, do we?" The girls had too many fun things planned to spare time for a summer trip.

"No..."

They all waited while he struggled to find the right words.

"Just tell them, Sam!" Sasha raised her voice, something she very rarely did, and then buried her face in her hands. She couldn't bear to watch what was about to happen.

"We're not going to visit California. We're moving there," Sam blurted.

"What do you mean?" Poppy asked. He might as well have been speaking Martian. His words did not compute.

"My mother isn't getting any younger. She wants to

spend time with her grandkids…"

"Then she should move here," Esme reasoned, cutting her father off mid-sentence.

"You didn't let me finish. The other thing, the bigger thing, is your mom has a really terrific job offer." Kay had been laid off from her teaching job a year earlier.

"Why can't she just get a job here?" Esme argued.

"You know she's been trying. And this is a great opportunity."

Kay finally spoke up, saying loudly, "Don't sugarcoat it, Sam!"

Not wanting to worry Esme and Grady, Sam and Kay had shielded their kids from how tough things were getting financially. But the decision was final, and everyone deserved to know why. Kay sat down on the edge of the wooden coffee table and took one shocked girl's hand in each of hers.

"Yes," Kay explained, "it is a wonderful opportunity to teach at a top-notch art school. That's true. I am excited about that. But it's also the only full-time position I've been offered. And the truth is, we simply can't afford my being out of work any longer."

Kay paused, and when no one jumped in, she added, "We're lucky. Sam can work from anywhere. And like he said, you should really get to know your grandmother better, Esme."

All Esme knew of Grandma Martha was that she liked to be called Marty, she had been a dancer before she started making costumes for the movies, and she sent weird Christmas presents, like used handbags and hats. Sasha and Kay always oohed and aahed over them, but the girls just thought they looked old and smelled funny.

"This is happening, girls. I'm sorry," Kay added sternly.

"But really, Esme, California is pretty great," Sam chimed in. "It's warm, and you can swim all year long."

Esme yanked her hand away from Kay's angrily.

Poppy remained perfectly still as if in a trance, her eyes darting back and forth as she processed the horrible news. She couldn't stand the thought of Esme leaving. She also remembered how hard it had been for them when Sasha was finishing law school and money was tight. She knew money wasn't the most important thing in life. But she also knew it was absolutely necessary.

Sasha caught Kay's eye and gestured toward the kitchen.

The two moms were together in the kitchen, quietly tidying up the last of the evening's mess, when an ear-splitting noise pierced the air.

"NOOOOOOOOOOOO!!!!!!!!!!" Esme stood in the center of the living room, her eyes squeezed shut, tears streaming down her now crimson cheeks.

Poppy stood behind her, crying softly, a look of disbelief on her face. "You can't. What about us?"

"Maybe this wasn't the best time to drop this news," Kay mumbled to no one in particular.

"No duh, Mom," Esme muttered. There was no good time for news this bad. "I'll just stay here with Poppy," she declared defiantly, looking to Sasha for confirmation she was welcome.

Poppy, who was now blubbering hysterically, nodded fiercely in agreement, sending tears and runny boogers flying everywhere.

Sasha's heart broke for the girls "Esme, you know you're always welcome, but..." She couldn't continue. She was too choked up.

"...we discussed that," Kay finished her friend's sentence. "If it was just through the end of a school year, or maybe if you two were older and it was the last year of high school..."

But it wasn't. It was the summer before middle school. The worst time ever to separate two best friends. This was so unfair!

"You can't make her go!" Poppy, usually the more subdued of the pair, shouted angrily through tears.

"Okay, everyone," Sam pleaded, his head throbbing from the hysterics, "Let's just take a minute, take a deep breath."

They heard the heavy deadbolt on the front door click. The girls looked at each other with hope in their eyes. No way Grady was going to stand for this.

At fourteen, Esme's brother was already the tallest one in the family, and his clothes were having trouble keeping up. His t-shirt hung loosely on his lanky frame, and his brand new skinny black jeans already looked too short. Skateboarding, friends, his appearance, and his phone were his primary interests.

Grady looked around the room with a neutral expression and muttered, "I see you told them."

How long had he known? Esme fumed to herself. *Older brothers are supposed to look out for younger sisters, not keep secrets from them!*

"Grady, why didn't you tell me?" Esme yelled.

"Now I'm going to be all alone," Poppy whined.

The girls continued their pleas for help so quickly and loudly it was impossible to decipher who was saying what.

"Hey, I'm not happy about it either," was all Grady said as he pulled his phone out of his pocket and disappeared past them into his room.

"This isn't going to be easy for anyone, girls," Sam pointed out. "But you'll have the whole summer together. And Poppy, you're going to love visiting us in California once we're settled. This really is a wonderful opportunity for your mom, Esme. You should be excited for her."

"Well, I'm not! I wish she would just go without us!"

And there it was. Esme could tell from the hurt look on her mom's face that she'd gone too far. She wished she could take it back, but it was too late. She ran to her room and slammed the door, leaving Poppy, still crying, in the living room with the adults. After a moment, Poppy took a deep breath, collected herself, walked to Esme's room, and knocked lightly.

"Es, it's me. It'll be okay," Poppy reassured her friend. "I'm coming in."

CHAPTER TWO

A Lightbulb Moment

Poppy hadn't slept a wink, and it showed. She glanced in the hallway mirror, frowned at her reflection, and tried to smooth her unruly brown curls before heading downstairs to the lobby to meet Esme. It was hopeless. Her hair was as tangled as her feelings.

As she sluggishly walked out of the elevator, thinking about the night before, Poppy felt a lump forming in her throat. She was a bundle of emotions—sad, angry, confused.

Just then, the stairwell door banged open loudly. Esme, pink in the cheeks from running down six flights of stairs, burst into the lobby. "This is so lame! I can't believe this is happening to us."

Poppy sniffled as she slipped on pink aviator sunglasses to cover her red, watery eyes.

Esme put her arm around Poppy and said, "Come on. Let's get out of here and go to the park. I think there's some circus festival happening today."

The girls stepped out into the mottled sunlight on the city sidewalk and headed toward Tompkins Square Park, just a couple of blocks away. Poppy turned back to their building and glanced up at the metal stars.

"Remember when your dad told us the truth about those stars?" Poppy asked.

"Oh man, we thought we lived in the star building because we were princesses or fairies or something special…" Esme sighed and launched into her spot-on imitation of Sam, who seemed to know a little bit about everything. "'Those aren't just for you girls. Each star is actually attached to an iron rod to help support the brick building and keep it from crumbling as it gets older.' He ruined everything that day. Just like he did last night."

"Well, they still look pretty. You probably won't have anything like them in California."

"I won't have the park either," Esme added sadly. "Tompkins is the best."

Tompkins Square Park took up a whole block and was the coolest park in the East Village. In addition to the grassy areas and paved walkways you'd expect to find, it also had a kids' pool, three playgrounds, ping-pong tables, handball courts, and a dog run. But most of all, it had tons of interesting people. The surrounding neighborhood was originally home to Russian, Jewish, and Ukrainian immigrants. Artists, musicians, hippies, and students moved in during the 1960s. Today, it was a mix of different cultures, lifestyles, nationalities, and backgrounds, and everyone enjoyed using the park.

"I think the people are the best thing about Tompkins," Poppy stated. "It's the best people-watching in the world." Poppy was extremely observant, like a really good spy or detective. She loved watching all the neighborhood characters and wondering about their lives.

"The people are the best thing about our whole neighborhood," Esme said as she waved to Tony and Elaine, who owned their favorite pizza place on the corner.

The East Village wasn't what most people think about when they imagine New York City. It wasn't just skyscrapers, crowded streets, and speeding taxi cabs. It was also a mix of small apartment buildings, cute shops, and friendly neighbors.

"Hey, Peonies!" Tony shouted. Tony always shouted. Not in a mad way. He just shouted all the time. "How'd we do on the special Peony Pizza last night? Was it the way you like it? Light on the sauce, heavy on the broccoli, am I right?"

"You guys did great, Tony. Better than ever!" Esme shouted back. The girls thought maybe Tony shouted because he was a little hard of hearing. She turned to Poppy and said, "At least we ate before they told us about California. I would have lost my appetite."

Drew's Diner on the corner was bustling. All of the outside tables were full. A line of people spilled out the door, most of them looking over menus, deciding between decadent waffles with whipped cream and fruit, Drew's famous cinnamon buns, or the New York City classic: bacon, egg, and cheese on a roll.

Through the windows, they could see black and white photos decorating the walls of the diner, all taken by Poppy's dad, Will. There were candid shots captured in the park and at the East River, and also elaborately staged scenes with models and costumes. Will was a pretty well-known professional photographer, and he'd been taking pictures of the girls since they were born.

"I never really thought about it before, but your dad's photos really capture the vibe of the neighborhood," Esme said. "Do you think he'd give me one for my room in Los Angeles?"

"Duh. And I'm sure he'll take a million more pictures of us this summer!"

"To add to the ten million we already have..."

"Remember his photo series 'It Takes a Fairy Village'?" Poppy recalled, pointing at one of her favorite photos hanging prominently above the cash register inside.

"That was the best," Esme smiled. "I never wanted to take off those wings!"

Poppy's father had the girls model fairy wings in super urban settings around the East Village when they were five. The wings were made of silver netting decorated with glistening rhinestones and glitter, and they hung effortlessly from the girls' shoulders by barely noticeable silver ribbons. People loved the contrast of beautiful fairies in front of a gritty chain link fence or leaning on a police car.

The photo above the cash register was taken at the Dry Dock public pool on 10th Street. Will had the girls jump on mini trampolines next to the pool while a lifeguard and all of the swimmers acted surprised. The picture made it look just like they were floating above the water, and they never even got wet.

"We even wore our wings to the gallery opening!" Esme remembered. "I thought I was a real city fairy."

"I didn't like being the center of attention, even then. I hid behind you the whole time," Poppy recalled.

"I loved it! Dad kept saying, 'You're just like your Grandma Marty, always in the spotlight!'"

Remembering all of the fun they had made the reality of the future even harder to take.

Up ahead, Julie's pink, star-shaped Lucky Stars sign beckoned to the girls like a lighthouse in the fog of the horrible news that was still sinking in.

"Let's stop in," Poppy suggested.

They waited for the light, looked both ways as always, just to be sure, and then bolted across the street toward their home away from home, and their stand-in older sister, Julie.

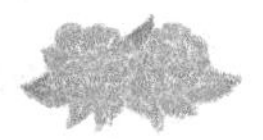

Bells jingled as they stormed through the door, startling Julie's tiny dog, Scribbles. He looked kind of like a toy poodle with puffy brown hair and beady black eyes, but Julie said he was more like a toy doodle because he definitely had a bunch of other breeds scribbled in. Scribbles leaped to his feet and charged toward them, but he yipped a greeting once he realized the intruders were friends, not foes. Scribbles had the personality of a giant German Shepherd guard dog in a miniature body, and he was used to getting his way.

Julie laughed. "Scribbles honestly believes he's protecting me and the shop. If only he knew he only weighs seven pounds! I've seen bigger rats on the subway tracks!"

"No way! The average New York rat only weighs between one and two pounds," Poppy protested as she scooped up Scribbles the Attack Dog and headed toward the counter.

The Lucky Stars counter was used for wrapping gifts and ringing up purchases on an old-fashioned cash register, but the four stools surrounding it made it perfect for girl talk and eating the occasional dinner. The shelves weren't normal store shelves; they were homemade, built out of driftwood Julie had collected on the beach, brought back into the city, reconditioned, and painted white. Antique furniture and knick-knacks were scattered throughout, little white lights hung everywhere, and there was always a fragrant candle burning. Julie's jewelry workbench was tucked back in the corner, littered with a mess of beads, metal wire, fixtures, wax molds, tools, and found objects, all of which somehow, in Julie's talented hands, turned into beautiful, wearable art. Her jewelry was expensive, too expensive for eleven-year-olds, but it wasn't locked up in a case. It was scattered amongst all the other merchandise, like treasures you had to search for. The shop was a magical place for the girls.

Esme made a beeline past the counter. Without looking, Poppy knew exactly where her best friend was headed. On a shelf in the corner, nestled in an old porcelain teacup filled with dried flower petals, were two gold pendants on fine gold chains. They were perfect, tiny peonies Julie had made, inspired by Poppy and Esme's friendship. In fact, the girls had inspired a whole line of spring flower pendants—in addition to peonies, there were roses, daisies, daffodils, and tulips. All of the other flower pendants had sold out, but the girls had been secretly hiding the peony necklaces for months. Julie made them with the girls in mind; it just didn't seem right for anyone else to wear them. But mostly, there was that small issue of cost—actually, at $175 each, $350 total, it wasn't a small issue at all. They had hoped their parents might get them the necklaces for their birthdays. But they weren't surprised when it didn't happen. $175 was a lot of money for grown-ups, too.

"I'm going to miss this place so much," Esme sighed as she fiddled with one of the pendants.

"Your mom told me she applied for a job in California, but I didn't know she got it," Julie said. Tears started to roll down Esme's face. "Oh, Es...So it's final? You guys are moving?"

"Yeah," Poppy said as she hugged her friend. She hated seeing anyone upset, especially Esme. "Our parents told us last night. It wasn't our best family dinner, that's for sure."

"Oh, come here, both of you...I can't imagine how you're feeling." Julie wrapped her arms around both girls. "Sit down, talk to me."

Julie cleared space on the counter, pushing aside some papers and a tangle of ribbon.

"It's just so unfair," Poppy exclaimed, "to split up our friend-family like this."

"Unfair to whom though? This is an awesome work opportunity for Kay; it'll be great for Esme to be close to her grandma; and you'll have somewhere cool to visit, Poppy."

"But what about us? Why couldn't she just find a job here?" Esme asked, banging her fists on the counter for emphasis.

"You know she's been looking, honey. There just aren't a ton of great jobs here right now for art professors."

"Why does she need a 'great' job? I see 'help wanted' signs everywhere. Why can't she just work somewhere in the neighborhood?" Esme waved her arms through the air and then crossed them stubbornly in front of her chest.

"Your mom is an amazing teacher. When I was in art school, she was EVERYONE'S favorite because she loves teaching. She deserves to have the chance to do what she loves. Change can be tough; I'm not going to pretend it isn't..."

Bells jingled and three older women walked through the door. They were all carrying "I LOVE NEW YORK" gift bags, a dead giveaway they were visiting from out of town. As the women looked around the shop in wonder, Scribbles started barking and bounded toward the door.

"Sorry, sorry...Scribbles, come on now! Welcome, ladies. Girls, can you do me a favor and take Scribbles for a little walk?"

The girls looked at each other in disbelief. Julie had never let them take Scribbles out by themselves before. They had been asking for years. "Sure thing," they said quickly, in unison.

"Just make sure he pees, and don't let him boss you around. You're in charge. Now, go, go..." Scribbles was still barking, and the customers were looking ready to bolt.

"I'm so sorry, ladies. The dog is leaving. Come on in. How can I help you?" Julie handed the leash to Esme and practically shoved them out the door.

"Well, that was awkward!" Esme said as she hooked Scribbles' leash to his harness.

"But at least we finally get to walk Scribbles," Poppy said. "Julie really needs to train him not to scare customers away."

"I wish we could train him to protect our peony necklaces until we can save enough money from our allowances to buy them."

As the girls thought about the pendants, Scribbles

tugged on the leash, sniffing frantically around the tree in front of Lucky Stars. He circled it. He scratched at the dirt. He looked back at the girls. He got distracted by the sound of someone pulling their suitcase down the sidewalk and started barking at the wheels. Then back to the tree to sniff it again. He sat down, stood up, and wagged his tail. The only thing he didn't do was pee.

"At this rate, we could be out here for an hour," Esme said, remembering what Julie had said about taking charge. "Come on, Scribbles, let's keep it moving!"

Scribbles moved, but it was slow going. Every leaf, chewed-up piece of gum, locked-up bike, and garbage can required a full investigation. Scribbles finally found the perfect spot next to a mailbox on the corner.

Now that his business was done, the girls meandered down the street, letting Scribbles take the lead. As they entered the park, their conversation was interrupted by the sound of slow clapping and a familiar voice.

"So, Julie finally trusted you two with Scribbles. Did you have to pay her or something?" There was Grady, strewn across a park bench next to his best friend, Nico. Their skateboards were at their feet.

"Whatever, Grady, it didn't take any convincing. Actually, she practically begged us," Esme retorted.

"Yeah," Poppy added, backing up her best friend.

"Leave them alone, G," Nico said, punching Grady in the arm. As the youngest in his family, Nico never got on board with Grady teasing them. He knew what it was like.

"What's up, Peonies?"

"Well...you know," Esme replied, glancing away from Nico shyly. She didn't have to look at him to know that his thick, dark brown hair was slicked back from his face. Or that his braces glistened in the sun when he smiled, and his big, deep-set brown eyes were focused on her. Nico was friendly, funny, and could connect with anyone, especially from the stage. He had starred as the Cat in the Hat in the eighth-grade production of *Seussical* and got a standing ovation all five nights. Grady had done lights for the show and told Esme that people lined up to congratulate Nico every night after the show. Esme totally understood. Nico was super talented and definitely the cutest boy she had ever seen, even in that goofy red and white striped hat.

"We should go, Es. Scribbles needs a little more exercise," Poppy said, saving Esme from the awkward silence. Normally, Esme could talk to anyone, anytime, but ever since seeing Nico's performance, she got completely tongue-tied around him.

"Right," Esme said quickly, pulling on the leash, "Come on, Scribbles. See ya later!"

"Let's do a quick spin through the park? See if we can find that circus festival?" Poppy suggested as they walked away.

To their left was the park's most popular grassy knoll, a lush green area with a gentle hill in the middle. It was surrounded by low rose bushes, patches of daffodils and irises, and about a million different varieties of hearty, leafy hosta plants. A few towering elm trees offered canopies of shade from the steaming summer sun. A college-aged guy played guitar while his friends sang along. Three moms, or maybe they were babysitters, chatted while their kids chased a ball around. Sunbathers in swimsuits stretched out on blankets, making do without a beach close by.

The sound of delighted whoops and splashes grew louder as the girls approached the busy kiddie pool. A lifeguard's whistle screeched and they smiled, knowing someone had just gotten in trouble for running on the slippery deck or dunking a smaller kid. The Peonies were glad they had graduated to the big Hamilton Fish public pool, which was a few blocks away, but happy they still qualified to pop into the kiddie pool when it was super hot and they needed a quick dip.

Two old men leaned on an iron fence, waving their hands in the air while having what seemed to be a spirited discussion. A woman quickly pushing a cart filled with groceries came toward them, and Scribbles barked and lunged at the squeaky wheels.

"Scribbles, no!" Esme said firmly, tightening her grip on the leash, "Mind your own business. This way."

"Good save, Es. I think he's got a thing about the sound of wheels. We'll have to watch that."

Finally, they found a small group of jugglers gathered on a lawn past some ping pong tables.

"Ladies and gentlemen, welcome to the smallest show

on earth," Esme said in her best P.T. Barnum voice. They watched for a few moments, but Esme quickly grew bored. "Hardly a 'festival.' Let's head back."

On the return trip, they passed the older women Scribbles had nearly chased out of the store—but now each held a pink Lucky Stars bag in her hand. Esme let go of the leash as they entered the shop.

"Hi, sweetie-pie! Come here! Did you miss your mama?" Julie baby talked as Scribbles leaped up into her lap. "Did he pee?"

"Mission accomplished," Esme confirmed, "and we saw your new customers!"

"Mission accomplished indeed!" Julie said, reaching up to high five the girls. "They were here with a group from Connecticut on a walking poetry tour. How cool is that? And they all bought something, too!"

"Thanks for trusting us with Scribbles. I think we did a really good job with him; once we got going, he knew who was in charge," Poppy added.

"I'm sure he did, and he seems very happy. Thanks for getting him out of here so I could make some sales! The rent doesn't pay itself." Julie reached into the cash drawer and handed Esme two dollars.

"In fact," Julie continued, "I was thinking we could work out a deal. It would be really helpful if I didn't have to close the shop to take Scribbles out a couple of times a day. I'm probably missing a few customers a week, and I need every sale."

Without even consulting each other, the girls agreed enthusiastically.

"TOTALLY!" Esme yelled.

"YES! YES!" Poppy agreed. "Esme, are you thinking what I'm thinking? We both love dogs, we took great care of Scribbles, and we deserve to do what we love, just like your mom! We should start a business."

Poppy calculated quietly in her head, thinking about the peony necklaces hiding in the corner, and mumbled to herself, "Hmmm...I wonder how many dogs we'd have to take on how many walks to earn $350..."

"That's a great idea, girls," Julie confirmed. "I'm not the only one who could use some help. Mr. Kent on the third floor in your building is having knee surgery next week. I don't think he has a plan for walking Precious."

Esme chimed in, "And we've hardly seen Chunky out and about since the twins were born." Chunky was the French bulldog who also lived in their building and whose owners, Liz and Ray, had newborn twins.

"What should we call it? East Village Dog Walkers?" Poppy asked, getting right down to business, as always, and blurting out the first thing that came to mind.

"Ummm...no bad ideas in brainstorming, but that's not very exciting. Keep thinking..." Esme encouraged.

"Canine Companions?" Poppy suggested.

"Too serious. Maybe Dog-ercize? Like exercise for your dog?" Esme said, jogging in place.

"I don't love it. Healthy Dogs? Never mind, sounds like

something made out of tofu."

"Maybe Puppy Love?" Esme batted her eyelashes.

"Cute, but it doesn't say what we do," Poppy tried again, "Wag-N-Walk?"

"Better...hmmmm...what about Tompkins Trotters?" Esme tried.

"I like where you're going with the alliteration. But it sounds like the name of a horseback riding club," Poppy reasoned. "WAIT. I've got it!! Drumroll please!"

Esme and Julie drummed their fingers on the counter.

"Introducing...PEONY'S PRANCING PUPS!"

CHAPTER THREE

Bark of the Town

Poppy could hear Esme yelling all the way down the hall as she got closer and closer to her door. The good thing was Poppy always knew when her best friend was coming. The bad thing was, so did all the neighbors. Esme had her own definition of "inside voice."

"POPPPPPPPPPYYYYYYYY! It's time! Poppppppp—"

Poppy flung the door open, stopping Esme's shriek mid-word.

"Es, the neighbors are definitely not going to miss you yelling for me once you move!" Poppy giggled as Esme bombed into the living room, plopped on the soft green couch, and snuggled into a pile of pillows. The layout of Poppy's apartment was exactly like Esme's four flights up, but with one less bedroom. It was cozy and inviting, filled with warm earth tones, natural wood, candles, and artwork by all of their parents' friends.

"Come on, Pop. Get your shoes on! Our puppies await."

Esme pretended to tap an imaginary watch on her wrist while Poppy pulled on her favorite silver boots.

"Perfect for a real businesswoman, don't you think?" Poppy asked and did a little spin, showing off her boots.

"Yes, but real businesswomen are on time! Let's go!" Esme urged, heading toward the front door.

"I guess we'll have to skip the blueberry muffins."

Esme stopped in her tracks.

"Mom got them for us from Corner Café as a special treat," Poppy said, pointing to a plate covered with tin foil on the kitchen counter.

"Well, real businesswomen also need nourishment," Esme said, peeling back the foil. It was impossible for her to resist a warm blueberry muffin. They were her favorite.

"How about we check our supplies while we eat?" Poppy suggested, handing Esme the list she prepared.

"Good thinking, Pops. Okay, let's see..." Esme began reading the items on Poppy's list off one by one in between bites of muffin.

"Water bottles?"

Poppy zipped open her backpack.

"Check. We must keep ourselves and our canine clients hydrated at all times."

"Definitely," Esme agreed. "Snacks?"

"Check. Two apples, string cheese, granola bars."

"Yum. Oooh. This is a good one...Sunscreen for me?"

"Got it. You know how you burn."

Esme smiled. Poppy was considerate even when she was in business mode.

"Mini notebook for you?"

Poppy nodded. "So I can keep a tally of all of our earnings."

"Good thinking. Poop bags for…poop?" Esme joked.

"Gross"—Poppy wrinkled her nose— "but yes, check. And plenty of hand sanitizer, too."

"Wow. You thought of everything, Poppy." Esme was impressed. "And don't worry, we'll take turns with the poop."

And with that, the girls grabbed their supplies, locked the door behind them, and raced up the stairs to the fifth floor.

Poppy and Esme stopped outside of apartment 5A, where they could hear the twins crying and Chunky barking through the door. They knocked and looked at each other knowingly. They would really be helping Liz out by walking Chunky. She could use one less noisy voice in the house.

Liz opened the door with a crying baby in each arm and Chunky trailing right at her heels. She bounced the babies gently and gestured for the girls to come in with a nod of her head.

"Hey, Peonies," she said. Her eyes were red and swollen from lack of sleep, and her voice, flat and low, had none of its normal energy. "Come on in. Forgive the mess."

Liz kicked aside some laundry, gently put the babies in matching bouncy chairs on the floor, and collapsed on a brown leather couch. Above it hung a huge framed poster featuring her favorite musician, David Bowie, who had a lightning bolt painted down the middle of his face. Liz wore a stretched-out vintage t-shirt from the famous rock club CBGB. Her bangs practically covered her eyes.

"And forgive my hair," Liz apologized again, running her hand through her short, slightly greasy tresses. "Would you ever believe I'm a hairstylist? Thank goodness my clients can't see me right now."

The girls had never seen Liz without perfectly styled hair before the twins. But she had become increasingly disheveled since her babies arrived two months earlier. After all, she literally had her hands full.

"Don't be crazy, Liz," Esme reassured her. "You always have the funkiest haircuts. You'd make David Bowie proud."

David Bowie was Liz's hair inspiration. Sometimes she wore it spiky on top and long in the back. Sometimes it was slicked straight back. Sometimes she brushed it forward like a pixie. The color was always a surprise, too.

"And what are we? Chopped liver?" Poppy objected. "I thought we were your favorite customers? I'd never let anyone else touch my hair! No one else knows how to deal with this mop." Poppy tousled her own thick, springy hair.

"Or how to add body and shine to my luscious locks." Esme flipped her sleek, straight hair dramatically.

"Aw, thanks, girls. You're making this bedraggled stylist feel better," Liz laughed. "You both have great hair."

Liz helped take care of the girls when they were babies and had been cutting their hair their whole lives. Sometimes, a little David Bowie style snuck in on the girls, too. They loved when that happened.

"The babies are so cute, Liz," Poppy said as she leaned over to pet Chunky, who was now squirming around their feet, not wanting to be left out of the action. "Don't worry, Chunk, you're cute, too!"

"Thanks, Poppy. All three of them are cute, but Chunky is a little bit jealous of his brothers, and he's driving me crazy! It's been tough lately with Ray on the road."

Liz's husband, Ray, was a sound guy who worked with the coolest rock and roll bands. Musicians loved working with Ray; he was easy-going and knew everything there was to know about sound gear. He could solve any problem that came up.

"Where is he?" Esme asked.

"Somewhere on the West Coast, sleeping on a tour bus with seven other crew members. It's not the best timing with the babies. But the show must go on."

"Well, actually, that's why we're here," Esme said. "We started a business—Peony's Prancing Pups, a dog walking service. Perfect for the coolest new mom in Manhattan!"

"And affordable, too. Just two dollars a walk. We'll get Chunky some exercise and get you some quiet time. We can reduce your noise by one-third," Poppy added, showing off her knowledge of fractions.

"Get the leash. You're hired." Liz didn't need any more convincing. She really needed the help.

"YAHOOOOOO!!!!" Esme yelled.

"ESME! IN. SIDE. VOICE," Liz and Poppy exclaimed at the same time.

"Sorry...yahooooooooooo!!!!" Esme whisper-screamed.

"We could take Chunky out twice a day? Morning and afternoon? Would that be good?" Poppy suggested.

"Heavenly," Liz sighed. "Starting immediately, please, so I can get the babies to sleep. And maybe trim my bangs, too."

The girls leaped into action. "C'mon, Chunk. Let's do this!" Esme said and grabbed the leash from a hook by the door.

Chunky knew what that meant. He bolted toward the door on his muscular little legs, wagging his stub of a tail.

"No rush getting back, Peonies. Take your time... please!" Liz begged.

The girls high-fived as they shut the door and headed to the elevator.

Esme pushed the elevator button with confidence and declared, "Next stop, Sir Charles. Third floor! Elevator going down. Watch your hands and feet."

"I just can't knock on his door, Es. You do it." Poppy cowered behind her taller friend as they got closer to apartment 3D.

"But Sir Charles likes you more! You're the good one. He thinks I'm a monster!"

"To be fair, he thinks anyone who doesn't know a salad fork from a dinner fork is a monster."

"Give me a break, Poppy...he taught us about forks in second grade. 'Pay attention now, children. You work your way in from the outside. Salad fork on the outside, dinner fork on the inside, next to the plate.'" Esme spoke in a deep voice and emphasized each word slowly. She did a pretty good imitation of Sir Charles.

"Esme, your enunciation is top drawer."

Esme smiled. She could mimic the way Sir Charles sounded when she tried, but Poppy sometimes repeated his fancy language and old-fashioned sayings without even realizing it.

"Sir Charles" was The Peonies' secret nickname for Charles Kent, an older gentleman who seemed more like a member of a royal family than someone from the East Village. He was very serious and formal and acted like the etiquette teacher for the whole neighborhood. Unfortunately for the girls, they ran into him almost every day—in the lobby, on the elevator, at the bodega...The Peonies were his favorite students.

Poppy and Esme felt like they had to be on their best behavior when he was around, or he'd have something to say about it. He always had some advice or piece of wisdom for them, even when they didn't ask for it:

"Look people in the eye when you talk to them."

"Be sure to wash your hands, girls. Good hygiene is paramount in the fight against spreading germs."

"Always make sure to look your best. It shows self-respect."

"You're young and able-bodied. You should offer your seat on the bus to your elders."

"No running through the halls unless something is on fire."

"If you can't say something nice, don't say anything at all."

Having someone always telling you what to do just wasn't that fun. Even his beloved Cavalier King Charles Spaniel, Princess Precious, didn't seem that fun.

"Listen, Esme, we have to go for the business," Poppy reasoned, always the sensible one. "Like Julie said, Sir Charles is having surgery on his knee next week. How can he walk Precious if he can't walk himself?"

"I know, I know..." Esme sighed.

The girls sheepishly approached the door. They had always tried to avoid Sir Charles, and they certainly hadn't ever knocked on his door before—not even trick or treating on Halloween. Any time Sir Charles saw the girls with a sweet treat, he'd say, "Now Peonies, too much sugar isn't good for growing children."

They looked at each other and without saying a word, shook their fists three times at each other, the final shake ending in a "rock" and "scissors."

"Sorry, Es," Poppy said. "Rock beats scissors. You knock."

Esme straightened her shoulders, hearing Sir Charles' voice in her head, "Mind your posture, girls." Poppy did the same.

Esme knocked softly.

Inside, Precious yipped hello, and they heard shuffling coming toward the door.

The girls nervously turned to face each other for a last-minute check. Poppy smoothed Esme's hair and tucked a few random pieces behind her ears, while Esme licked her finger and rubbed at a mystery spot on Poppy's shirt.

"Ew. Poppy. Is this from your breakfast or the babies?"

The door swung open and there stood Sir Charles, peering down over his bifocals at the girls, his thin, wrinkled lips turned down in what seemed like a permanent frown. As always, he was impeccably dressed—"dapper," as Esme's mom called it—in a silky paisley robe over navy blue cotton pajamas. On his feet, he wore red velvet slippers embroidered with King Charles Spaniels.

In his arms was his very old spaniel, Princess Precious. Her brown and white coat was perfectly groomed, and there was a navy-blue bow in her long fur to match his pajamas. Sir Charles always coordinated her bows to match his ensemble.

The girls knew it wasn't nice, but the matching accessories made them giggle almost as much as Sir Charles having a King Charles Spaniel named Princess Precious.

"Well, good morning, girls. To what do I owe the honor of your visit? I do believe it's the first time The Peonies have ever graced my door with their presence. And I see you've brought company."

Chunky barked as if on cue.

"Ummmm, well..." Poppy stammered when Esme didn't speak up. They had never seen him out of his normal uniform: a full suit and bowtie with a matching handkerchief tucked in his pocket, his white hair always neatly slicked back.

"Poppy, come now, we have discussed this time after time. Speak clearly; you need to enunciate your words and speak with confidence."

"Ummmm...Sir, umm, Mr. umm, Charles, no...Mr. Kent, yes, Mr. Kent, we'd like to talk to you about Precious."

Esme finally jumped in. "Julie mentioned you are having an operation. We started a dog walking business, as you can see," she said as she gestured to Chunky. "It's called Peony's Prancing Pups. We thought we could walk Precious for you while you recuperate. Just two dollars a walk."

"How very industrious of you children. But aren't you a little young to have started a business?"

"Well, we're in double digits now. We're both eleven and going to middle school next year. And we know everyone in the neighborhood in case we need help," Poppy reasoned, regaining her composure.

"Eleven, oh my. You're practically teenagers." Sir Charles said mockingly. "My Precious is a teenager as well. She's fourteen; that's ninety-eight in human years."

The girls snuck a glance at each other, both wondering if Sir Charles was also ninety-eight in human years. Esme stifled a smile.

He continued, "Her advanced age means she requires some special attention—sometimes her little legs get tired, and you have to carry her."

"Not a problem at all. Special attention is our middle name," Esme chimed in.

"It is true that I have yet to make arrangements," he admitted. "But I don't know..."

Sir Charles was turning out to be a tough customer.

"We're right here in the building in case of emergency or last-minute schedule changes," Esme added.

"And we could always bring coffee or something from the diner while we're out, you know, just while you're healing," Poppy improvised, trying anything to convince him.

"Hmmm, you do make some excellent points. And the fee is reasonable."

The girls held their breath and waited.

"What do you think, Precious?" Sir Charles scratched under the dog's chin.

She looked up at him, licked his face, and barked.

Chunky barked, too, and Precious started to wiggle toward him, which seemed to seal the deal.

"Well, I suppose we could give it a trial run. I can see you have one happy customer already."

"Two, actually." Esme was proud of their growing business. "We're picking up Julie's dog Scribbles on our way to the park. Thank you so much, Sir...umm...Mr. Kent. We'll take great care of Precious."

Sir Charles plucked a gold leather leash studded with glittering rhinestones from a porcelain bowl and fastened it to Precious' matching golden harness. He handed Precious and her leash to Esme.

As they stepped out into the hall, he called after them, "Take good care of her. Don't make me regret this decision, young ladies."

"Oh, you won't. She's going to have a great walk. Thanks again."

"No, thank YOU. Your new business will surely make life a little easier for Sir Charles."

And with that, he bowed slightly, gave the girls a big, dramatic wink, smiled, and closed the door.

The girls stared at each other in shock and ran off toward the elevator. Poppy anxiously pushed the button over and over. "Oh my gosh," she whispered, "he KNOWS we call him Sir Charles!!"

Esme whispered back, "But he winked! And SMILED... I've never seen him smile before."

The elevator arrived just then. The girls jumped in, and as soon as the doors shut, they both shrieked, startling the dogs.

"Maybe he actually does have a sense of humor?" Esme wondered.

"We'll find out," Poppy said, "but now we need to focus on our pups!"

The old elevator landed with a clunk, and the girls and dogs ran through the familiar lobby, burst onto the sidewalk, and headed toward Julie's shop. Chunky and Precious trotted along, clearly happy to be out and about with a buddy.

When Poppy, Esme, Precious, and Chunky arrived at Lucky Stars, they found two gifts—wrapped identically in pink leopard print paper with hot pink bows—on the counter. Julie had the best wrapping paper in town.

"For you," Julie said.

"For us?" Poppy marveled.

"Ooooh! First day of business gifts?!" Esme bounced on the balls of her feet.

"Exactly!" Julie, eager to see their reactions, handed

one to each. "Go ahead. Open them."

The girls tore open their packages to find folded, matching pink t-shirts, one size medium, one size small.

"Hold them up," Julie urged.

When they did, the shirts opened up to reveal a delicate peony design, just like the flower on the necklaces, and the words Peony's Prancing Pups in glitter lettering. They were beautiful.

"Did you make these yourself?" Poppy was amazed.

"They look so professional!" Esme chimed in.

"I wasn't sure if it should be Peony's with an apostrophe *s* or Peonies' with the apostrophe after—"

"We love them!" Esme cut her short. Who cares about details when you have your own uniform?

"Oh good! Now put them on and get out of here. I have a custom necklace I need to finish up by five."

The girls handed all three leashes to Julie and ran back to the tiny bathroom at the back of the shop to change.

Minutes later, they were proudly prancing their pups through the park toward the fenced-in section where dogs could play off-leash.

CHAPTER FOUR

Dogs' Day Out

Suzanne, the unofficial mayor of the dog run, stood just inside the gate, playing fetch with her rescue pitbull, Madeline. Madeline was fifty pounds of muscle and afraid of her own shadow. Suzanne had red hair with purple streaks and green eyes. She was both beautiful and terrifying.

"Hello, Scribbles. Hello, Chunky. Hello, Precious." Suzanne spoke to dogs more often than people.

"Hi, Suzanne!" The Peonies sang in stereo.

"Oh. It's the East Village Fairies," Suzanne said, startled as she acknowledged the dog's companions for the first time.

"That's us," Poppy smiled, trying to sound confident.

"Well, what's going on here, girls?" Suzanne demanded sternly, pointing to the dogs.

"We have a new business," Esme explained proudly, pointing at her t-shirt. "Peony's Prancing Pups. Two dollars per walk. Maybe we can help with Madeline sometime?"

Suzanne furrowed her brow at the ridiculous suggestion. Nobody walked Madeline but Suzanne, and she certainly didn't need any help, with anything, ever.

Madeline ran up and dropped a slobbery tennis ball at Suzanne's feet.

"Good girl!" She rubbed the dog's head and tossed the ball.

Scribbles and Chunky strained against their leashes with excitement. Esme reached for the gate, unlatched it, and started to push, but Suzanne blocked the way. Precious, seeming to sense the drama, sat down to watch the show.

Uh oh. Suzanne couldn't actually deny them access, could she? She took really good care of the dog run—refilling the poop bag dispenser, returning lost toys—but she didn't have any official power. Or did she?

"How much time have you spent with each of these dogs outside of the park?"

While Poppy calculated time spent with each dog in her head, Esme blurted, "Oh, tons!"

"And you know the rules of the run?" She pointed to the clearly posted rules.

They nodded. Of course they did. They could read.

"Three dogs. Two kids. Are you sure you can handle it?"

Now Poppy was getting annoyed. Of course they could handle it. She looked to Esme, who just smiled up at Suzanne confidently and replied, "Yep, we've got this handled."

Suzanne stepped aside and opened the gate. Apparently, they'd passed her test.

"Scribbles is going to want to play with the big dogs. Thor"—she pointed to an enormous black and tan dog whose head was bigger than Scribbles' whole body—"is his favorite. Liz always keeps Chunky in the small dog run. But she probably already told you that. And I'll give you *each* two dollars if you can get Precious to socialize with anyone."

And with that burst of unsolicited advice delivered, Suzanne turned her attention back to playing fetch with Madeline, but kept a close eye on the Peonies as they entered the dog park for the first time.

It was a lot less fun to split up, but they had a business to run, and they couldn't blow it on the first day. So Esme brought Chunky to the special small dog area while Poppy, Scribbles, and Precious stayed behind.

Poppy watched anxiously as Thor flipped a wriggling Scribbles around with his mouth. She didn't know which human he belonged to and couldn't help feeling nervous. Suzanne said the two dogs were friends. But still, Thor could snap Scribbles in half with one bite. She stood for five full minutes, glancing between the dogs and the humans. There were clusters of adults talking and drinking coffee, but none of them paid much attention to Poppy or the dogs. Maybe Thor's owner just dropped him off? Did people do that? Because it was hot standing in the sun and the dogs seemed okay playing, Poppy found a shady bench close by where she and Precious could observe the scene more comfortably, while still being close enough to react.

"Don't worry. They do that all the time," said an older gentleman with a cane as he approached and gestured to the bench. "May I?"

Poppy had seen him talking to Suzanne before, but she didn't know his name. He wore khaki Bermuda shorts, a wildly colorful red and pink, short-sleeved floral Hawaiian shirt, white socks, and pink plastic clogs.

Poppy knew not to talk to strangers, but Suzanne was only a few feet away.

Precious reached her head up toward the man, who rewarded her with a scratch behind her ears. "Hi, Precious. Good girl."

She'd never seen Precious do that to anyone but her owner.

"Precious and I are good friends. Aren't we, girl?" She licked his hand happily. "Charlie knows you have her, right?" he whispered to Poppy.

Charlie? Poppy thought. *Oh! Sir Charles!*

She smiled and nodded, "Oh yes," and then tentatively added, "I like your shoes."

He winked at her as if to say anyone who appreciated his fashion sense was okay with him.

Twenty feet away, in the small dog run, a pack of little dogs yapped and jumped around Esme. Suzanne was striding toward the scene to investigate.

"She gave the white one a treat in front of the others," he smiled. "I saw it on my way in. Rookie mistake. She's going to get an earful from Suzi for getting them all worked up."

Poppy couldn't help but laugh. Poor Esme.

"That's mine over there." He lowered himself onto the bench carefully and pointed to a fluffy black, white, and brown dog running gracefully in circles around the others.

"She's a cutie."

"He. His name is Tab, named after the old Hollywood heartthrob, not the diet soda. You're too young to remember either one."

"Doesn't he get dizzy running in circles?"

"Not at all," he laughed. "Tab's an Australian Shepherd. They're bred to herd cattle. No cattle in New York City, so he herds the other dogs."

"Really? That's so cool!"

He nodded, smiling.

"He ended up in a shelter because his owners didn't have time to take him out for exercise. I probably should have gotten a less active dog," the man said as he tapped his cane on the ground, "but I have plenty of time to watch him run around. And I just fell for him the second I met him."

Poppy liked the way he talked about Tab. She believed dogs all had their own personalities, too.

"He keeps me company and I make sure he gets lots of time to run around."

"Come on, Poppy! Let's gooooo!" Esme appeared out of nowhere, annoyed. "I've been calling you for, like, ten minutes." Chunky and Precious were happy to be reunited and nuzzled playfully at Esme's feet.

Poppy knew that was an exaggeration but let it slide.

"Okay, okay."

Both Suzanne and Tab's owner said Scribbles and Thor were friends, but Poppy was still a little cautious as she gently wrestled Scribbles out of Thor's mouth. The tiny dog's puffy brown hair was matted down with slobber, but he did seem happy. She clipped on his leash and did a quick headcount of the dogs. Came in with three. Leaving with three. So far, their first day was going pretty well.

"Will he be all right?" Poppy asked the man, nodding toward Thor. She didn't like the idea of just leaving him.

"Oh yes. His mom is never far," he assured her.

"Nice to meet you..." She didn't know the colorful man's name.

"I'm Todd. Tell Charlie I'll see him later."

"I will," Poppy promised.

"And *you*, young lady," he said to Esme. "Don't let Suzanne intimidate you. Her bark is much worse than her bite."

The girls waved goodbye and walked toward the exit, dodging stray balls and happy dogs. Esme lifted the handle on the heavy iron gate and held it open for Poppy.

As soon as they were out of earshot, Esme whispered dramatically, "Who's Charlie?"

Poppy laughed, linked her arm through Esme's, and leaned in close to fill her in.

CHAPTER FIVE

Stop, thief!

The girls raced down their busy block, each holding one end of a white plastic laundry basket, piles of folded clothes bouncing dangerously from side to side. On top of the pile were their Peony's Prancing Pups t-shirts, faded from being washed so many times over the past three weeks.

"Slow down or all of our hard work will be for nothing," Poppy pleaded. It felt like she was always begging Esme to slow down.

"So what! I've never understood folding clothes. It's like making the bed. A total waste of valuable time!" Esme swerved to avoid knocking into a tall, bearded man wheeling an enormous upright bass.

"You're going to get us killed, Esme!"

Every Fourth of July, for as long as Poppy and Esme could remember, their entire block shut down from corner to corner for an epic party. It was officially hosted by the public library, under the supervision of the local branch's head librarian, Ms. Borden, and was a celebration of the diversity and spirit of their beloved East Village. This year was the first time the girls were allowed to attend without a grown-up.

The block was bustling with activity. Food trucks and carts, offering everything from authentic Salvadoran pupusas to Korean barbecue tacos, lined the north side of the street. Wooden carts full of used library books—all for sale, cheap—filled a truck-sized gap in the middle of the action where tables and chairs were set up for relaxing and eating. A row of booths selling clothing, knickknacks, artisanal foods, and exotic spices ran along the sidewalk on the south side of the street. Later, they would find Julie in her booth at the end of the block. Lucky Stars always got great placement right in front of the stage.

"Hurry up, Poppy," Esme urged. "We have to get into our official tees and out on the street so we can drum up more business!"

Esme was right. The block party was the perfect opportunity to spread the word about Peony's Prancing Pups.

Just a few weeks into their enterprise, with seven weeks left until Esme's departure, the girls had already made almost half of the money for their necklaces. But they also had expenses—poop bags, bottled water, the occasional pizza slice, or passionfruit iced tea. And once Sir Charles was on his feet again, he'd be cutting back from two walks per day to one. If her math was right, and Poppy's math was always right, it would be a good idea to secure a few more canine customers, just to make sure they reached their goal in time.

Esme had the building key out and ready. They raced inside, up the stairs to 2B, and arrived just as Liz was opening the front door of Poppy's apartment.

"I thought I heard you."

Liz's bangs were trimmed, and her flawless makeup included smoky black eyeshadow and dark red lipstick. Her shiny black leggings and David Bowie t-shirt were, as of that moment, baby-mess free.

"You look beautiful!" Poppy complimented as the girls pushed past her into the apartment.

"Thanks. Your mom watched the babies while I primped for the block party."

"Hi, Sasha!" they called in unison as they ran past Poppy's mom and into her room. Sasha didn't love it when her own kid called her by her first name, but it was pretty cute when the girls shouted it out together.

In a flash, The Peonies were back in the living room, proudly sporting their matching tees.

"We've got Chunk, Liz." Esme grabbed the little dog's leash, pulling it taut against his bristly white hair. Chunky leaped up and followed on his stubby legs, leaving Sasha, Liz, and the twins in their double-wide stroller, behind.

"See you out there," Poppy called as she carefully pulled the door shut behind them.

They had no luck convincing Sir Charles to let them take Precious out—even when they offered to take her free of charge.

“Into that crowd? Really, ladies, I’m shocked you’d ask,” he scolded, clutching Precious to his chest.

Time to hit up Julie. The more dogs they could parade through the block party, the better for business.

Every year, Julie managed to transform an ugly booth at the end of the street into a magical mini version of Lucky Stars. This year was no different. Rows of tiny white lights lined the inside of the fabric walls. Tables covered with layers of scarves—sheer chiffon, printed silk, embossed velvet—held scented candles, handmade soaps, and beautiful cloth journals. Mismatched dishes that Julie had picked up from flea markets were scattered about, each containing one of her glittering or bejeweled masterpieces. Esme and Poppy waited patiently while she finished up a sale. Less patient, Chunky and Scribbles strained against their leashes trying to get to each other.

“Hi, Julie!” Esme waved.

“How’s business?” Poppy added.

“Great!” Julie stood up to reveal her ensemble: a long, lavender embroidered dress she also happened to sell at the store, styled with a thick chain necklace and her signature motorcycle boots. The lights created a halo effect around her mane of curly hair and reflected off her sparkly purple eyeshadow. She looked like a punk rock fairy.

Scribbles immediately took advantage of the lack of weight and dragged Julie's empty chair toward Chunky. His mess of untidy curls quivered as he used all of his strength to pull. He managed to move it a whole two inches.

"Can we take Scribbles?" Esme asked.

"Trying to drum up some new customers?"

They smiled and nodded. Julie understood them. She was a businesswoman, too.

"Do you have cards?"

Poppy pulled out a stack of twenty handmade business cards. Peony's Prancing Pups and Sam's cell phone number were written carefully in Poppy's very best handwriting. Each card also featured a peony flower drawn with a pink glitter pen.

"Gorgeous!" Julie approved.

She lifted up the chair, slid the end of Scribbles' leash off the leg, and handed it over along with the shiny black puppy purse she sometimes used to carry him around.

"He's all yours. Just be careful. There are more people on the street than he's used to, and it's easy for him to get under foot. Put him in his carrier if things get too crazy. And keep a close eye on him if you do. He sometimes tries to wriggle out."

Poppy and Esme worked their way slowly down the street, calling out, "Peony's Prancing Pups. Just two dollars a walk," and handing cards to anyone with a dog along the way. Halfway down, they cut through the seating area and onto the sidewalk in front of the library display.

Elaine from the pizza place was browsing through the books. She was holding identical blue nylon leashes attached to identical shaggy, long-haired yellow puppies.

"Hello, Peonies."

The puppies lunged in their direction, straining against their leashes.

"Ooooh! They're so cute!" Esme squealed, bending down to pet the pups. They knew Tony and Elaine were thinking about adopting a dog, but they weren't expecting two adorable little puppies.

The puppies licked Esme's hand with their long pink tongues and then turned their attention to Chunky and little Scribbles who, despite being a full-grown dog, was only about half their size.

"What kind are they?" Poppy asked, observing that the puppies looked a little like Golden Retrievers, but their snouts were shorter, and their coats were less thick.

"Honest to goodness, American mutts, fresh from the rescue on 38th Street."

"They're so sweet," Esme commented, watching them roughhouse with Chunky and Scribbles playfully.

The puppies were a blur of oversized paws and wagging tongues. Chunky was holding his own but Poppy was worried they might be a little too rough for Scribbles. She picked him up and slipped him into his carrier, just to be safe. Elaine nodded approvingly.

"They're a bit of a terror, actually," she confided. "They have so much energy."

"Well," Esme saw an opportunity and grabbed it. "I don't know if you've heard"—she proudly pointed at her shirt—"but we've started a business. We'll walk them, we'll play with them, we'll tire them out!"

"That's right," Poppy chimed in, handing Elaine a business card.

"Tony mentioned it. I'll definitely keep you girls in mind."

Elaine pulled on the puppy's leashes, called, "Come on boys," and started to walk away.

"Oh!" Esme called out, "What are their names?"

"Why, Meatball and Macaroni, of course!" The dogs jumped up in the air excitedly at the sound of their names.

As Elaine and the dogs disappeared into the crowd, a breeze blew in from the direction of the food vendors. It smelled like a delicious mix of spices, meats, and one of Esme's favorites, fried dough.

"Oooh! We should get funnel cakes!" Esme loved all sweets and baked goods—both eating and making them. She and Kay had watched cake decorating videos on YouTube last spring and made fancy cupcakes for the school bake sale. Ever since then, she was hooked.

Esme counted her stack of business cards while visions of funnel cakes danced in her head. "I only have four cards left. You?"

"Two," Poppy answered, distracted by a book display. "Here, hold him for a minute."

She handed Scribbles' carrier to Esme and opened up

an enormous hardcover book about horses.

"Let's get snacks, bring them back to your place, and make more cards. There's going to be a huge crowd when Evil Kitty Club hits the stage. It'll be the purrrr-fect time to pass them out."

Poppy shook her head and didn't even look up or acknowledge Esme's joke.

"A funnel cake is six dollars, Esme. We're supposed to be making money, not spending it. Besides," she said as she flipped the page, "you know I don't care for sweets."

It drove Esme a little bit crazy when Poppy said that. First of all, "I don't care for sweets," sounded fine coming out of Sir Charles' mouth, but ridiculous when repeated by her eleven-year-old friend. And second, she did too like sweets—particularly ice cream—just not as much as Esme did.

"Then you get something else. Let's each take ten dollars and get anything we want. We've earned it!"

To her surprise, Poppy didn't argue. "Okay, fine. You get a funnel cake. I'm going to get this book, and then I'll catch up and pick out my snack."

"Okay, but you'd better hurry up," Esme joked. "Evil Kitty Club goes on in two hours."

When given the opportunity to choose something for herself, Poppy always took forever to make a decision.

Poppy spent another ten minutes looking through books before she settled on the horse book she'd been looking at (one dollar and fifty cents), a gardening book with plenty of photos of peonies (one dollar), and a beat-up paperback story with drawings called *The Secret World of Og* (fifty cents). She paid Ms. Borden for her treasures, secured them in her backpack, and set off to find her friend.

Poppy caught up to Esme standing in front of the "We Fry It" truck, Chunky by her side, half a funnel cake in hand, lips covered with powdered sugar. "I couldn't wait," she said, smiling.

Esme looked at Poppy. Poppy looked at Esme. Something was wrong...What was it?

Poppy's heart jumped in her chest. Scribbles' carrier was turned upside down and empty on the ground under a table.

"Where's Scribbles, Esme?"

"I just set him down..." Esme looked at the table, then around it, then under it. "He was right here, Poppy."

Oh no! Esme had been so caught up in her snack, she'd taken her eye off of Scribbles. Poppy couldn't believe it. Julie told them this could happen.

"We've got to find him before he gets squashed," Poppy worried.

Esme tossed her half-eaten funnel cake in the nearest trash can. "And definitely before Julie finds out."

"We should ask around." Poppy started to approach a family seated nearby when Esme grabbed her.

"No way! Let's just see if we can find him first."

Poppy shook her head disapprovingly. "This is a serious situation. Es..."

"I know it is," Esme agreed. "But so is losing Julie's trust, and possibly getting grounded for the entire rest of summer. Just five minutes, then we'll start asking. Please?"

Poppy was torn. She knew they should get help right away. But five minutes wasn't so long. And it would be so much better if they could find Scribbles themselves. Not just for their friendship with Julie, and their summer, but for the business too. A lost dog would be terrible publicity, even if he was a known escape artist.

They navigated between the tables, looking for any sign of the tiny dog. No luck.

They crouched on the street, Esme looking west and Poppy east, between people's feet. No Scribbles.

Panic rising in her chest, Poppy was about to insist they admit their foul up and enlist some help when she caught a flash of tiny brown pouf out of the corner of her eye.

Across the tables, at a yellow and green food cart, Scribbles was balancing on his hind legs, jumping up excitedly at something out of Poppy's sight. He landed, and with his teeth clenched around the end of a hot dog at least twice his size, started dragging it through the crowd of waiting customers. The hot dog flopped from side to side and bounced off the sidewalk as the pleased puppy-thief wrestled it along.

"Look!" Poppy pointed.

Esme nodded, and without another word, the girls split up, slowly approaching Scribbles from opposite sides. Once Esme was ten feet behind him, she started closing in more quickly. Poppy, farther away and afraid to draw any attention by calling his name, tried to will Scribbles to look up at her. If they could just grab him without anyone noticing...

Too late. A little girl they didn't know, around four years old, tugged at her mom's skirt, "Mommy, look at the funny dog!"

From where Poppy stood with Chunky, it was as if the scene was moving in slow motion. The crowd parted. The little girl's mom picked her up. Adults started looking around for the dog's owner. And then, as if on cue, Esme swooped in and grabbed Scribbles, along with his hot dog. Thank goodness!

"I know. I know. That's a lot of hot for a little dog," Esme said to the mother and child with a smile. "But at Peony's Prancing Pups, we follow our clients' orders. You say get him a hot dog. We get him a hot dog."

With that, she pulled three dollars from her pocket, handed it to the still-startled vendor, thanked him, and ran to meet her friend.

"Great job, Es! But a lot of hot for a little dog?" Poppy laughed. "That doesn't even make sense."

Esme shrugged. "I'm just glad Scribbles didn't get lost forever."

"Or worse. He could have been hurt."

Now that the crisis was over, and reality was setting in, the girls realized just how serious the situation had been.

"I'm really sorry, Poppy. That wasn't very professional of me."

"Well, I probably shouldn't have suggested we split up," Poppy offered. Scribbles was her responsibility too, after all.

Esme tried to smile, but she was still upset.

"Don't worry Es. Everything turned out okay. And Scribbles wasn't exactly innocent in all of this either."

"Good point," Esme patted the naughty pup's head and set him down carefully next to Chunky, who licked Scribbles' entire hot dog-flavored face with his big slobbery tongue.

"Ewwwww!" Both girls exclaimed at once. "Gross!"

CHAPTER SIX

Wheels Up

Esme sulked in the corner of the big blue couch, twirling her hair and pretending to read her book. She was in a funk and wasn't trying to hide it from Kay and Julie, who were huddled together at the kitchen table sipping coffee and poring over sketches of new jewelry ideas. Julie had counted on Kay's feedback since art school, and she was prepping for an upcoming gift show. Esme let out a big, dramatic sigh to get their attention.

"Oh, for goodness' sake, Esme," Kay scolded. "It's not the end of the world."

"Well, what am I supposed to *do* all day?"

"Read your book, go to the park, draw, maybe clean your room?" Kay responded.

"Oh, that sounds fun," Esme replied sarcastically, "especially all alone."

"Poppy has a jujitsu competition today, so poor Es has to fend for herself for an entire day," Kay explained to Julie.

"Um, if this is how she's going to act without Poppy, I'd trade her in for another kid," Julie teased, shifting Scribbles on her lap. "You're going to have to start getting used to doing things on your own or with other kids, Es." Scribbles started barking as if he was agreeing with her.

Julie wasn't saying it to be mean, but she had a point. And, yes, it was the reason Esme was in such a bad mood today. But it wasn't just about today—being without Poppy today was just driving home how different things were going to be without her. It was coming out as bratty, but really, Esme was just sad and scared. She sighed again. This time for real.

Grady's bedroom door opened and he stumbled into the living room, still half asleep.

"Ten forty-five! I thought you were going to sleep all day!" Kay said, glancing at the clock on the wall.

"I could have, but the barking woke me up. Do we have anything for breakfast?" Grady asked as he walked into the kitchen. "I'm starving."

"We had breakfast at seven-thirty," Esme snapped, "when normal people wake up."

"What's your problem?" Grady asked. "I'm a growing boy. I need my beauty sleep."

Esme rolled her eyes and watched Grady pull a cereal box off the top shelf. She wondered how much taller he could possibly get.

"Oh, I have an idea," Julie said suddenly. Esme perked up; maybe Julie was going to suggest going on an excursion to South Street Seaport or a matinee or the Museum of Modern Art.

“Maybe, if I added a few more rings and combined the metals…wait, let me show you.” Julie picked up a pencil and tried to lean over the table. “Scribbles, move. I’m trying to work.”

Esme deflated. It was just an idea about jewelry design.

“He can really get in the way for being so little,” Julie said, putting Scribbles down on the floor. “Es, can you call him?”

“Scribbles, come here, buddy…” Esme said without much enthusiasm.

But Scribbles wasn’t having it today. He didn’t want to lose his cozy, prime spot on Julie’s lap. He stood on his hind legs with his front paws on Julie’s leg and started barking.

“I don’t blame you, Scribbles. *Dismay* is no fun when she’s in a mood,” Grady said, using the mean, but accurate, nickname he called Esme whenever she got in a funk. Esme glared at him.

“It’s not nice, but if the shoe fits…” Julie remarked.

“Guys, please knock it off,” Kay said, “we’re trying to work.”

“Scribbles, you too! Knock it off,” Julie said. He was still barking at her to pick him back up, but Julie wasn’t giving in.

“Mom, tell him not to call me that,” Esme said.

“Tell her not to be filled with so much dismay!” Grady responded.

"Mom, seriously!" Esme begged.

"'Mom, seriously!'" Grady repeated, imitating her perfectly.

"Okay. Enough," Kay said sternly. "Grady, get dressed. You and Esme are going to the farmers market in Union Square. And you're taking Scribbles."

"Mom, NO!" Esme and Grady said together.

"That's what you get. Don't mess with Kay," Julie said, laughing.

"We need some veggies for dinner and I need you out of our hair. You're going."

"Whatever," Grady mumbled and skulked back into his room.

"Get dressed!" Kay yelled.

"I am!" Grady yelled right back.

Esme stomped toward the front door where she had tossed her sneakers and her backpack. This was so annoying. She loved going to Union Square—there were lots of bigger stores, artists selling their work, people playing chess, and the huge farmers market, and it was farther away than she was allowed to go by herself. But going with Grady when she was already in a terrible mood? That was the worst thing in the world.

"Here's his leash," Julie said, winking at Esme. Esme managed a meager smile.

"Let's see...tomatoes, cucumbers, greens for salad..." Kay wrote a list on the back of one of the discarded sketches. She handed it, along with some cash, to Esme as

Grady emerged from his room, skateboard in hand.

"That's not going to work, Grady," Esme said knowingly. "Scribbles hates anything with wheels."

"She's right, I'm afraid," Julie chimed in. "You think he's being annoying now..."

"And the point is you need to walk with your sister," Kay said sternly, "not skate. Do you have your phone?"

"Obviously. And yes, Mom, I understand," Grady said. "I'll take my chances with Scribbles. There is some sick skating by the market."

Esme looked at Julie and shrugged as if to say, "We tried to tell him."

"You'll figure it out..." Julie called to Grady as the two kids and Scribbles walked out the door. "Just don't say we didn't warn you."

Esme, Grady, and Scribbles walked in silence for five or six blocks. Scribbles was so excited to be on a walk that he was blissfully unaware of anyone's bad mood.

"So, not that I really care, but why are you being such a buzzkill today?" Grady asked.

"Poppy has a jujitsu competition all day, so I'm stuck hanging out with you," Esme replied.

"You're being such a baby, Es. You've spent plenty of time without Poppy. You spend hours working on your dumb dance routines or doing stupid crafts. You do it all the time."

"I'm not being a baby," Esme objected, "and it's not just today."

Grady took several steps before replying.

"Dude, listen. I totally understand—you're not the only one who's moving—but you're being kind of selfish."

"But I'm leaving my best friend!" She stared right at Grady, who stared back in disbelief.

"Um, hello?? Me and Nico? Mom and Sasha? Dad and Will? We are all leaving our best friends."

Esme had been so caught up in her own feelings, she hadn't thought much about anyone else's. She looked down at the ground. Maybe it was a little selfish.

"And listen, besides that, Mom and Dad have a ton of other stuff going on. Figuring out the move, Mom planning for her new job, Dad dealing with all our school stuff...It doesn't help to have you moping around all the time."

"I just get so sad sometimes."

"No kidding, Dismay," Grady teased, "but you've got to rally and be cool. It makes Mom and Dad feel really bad."

"Did they tell you that?" Esme asked, alarmed. She didn't want to make anyone feel bad.

"Not exactly, but you can tell from their faces that they feel super guilty you're bummed out."

"I'm not just bummed out," Esme continued cautiously. She wasn't sure if she should admit this to Grady. "I'm really scared."

"Of a new school? Dude, you're going to be fine. Not that I noticed, but you have tons of friends, not just Poppy. And, I mean, it makes no sense to me, but kids seem to like you."

Esme stuck her tongue out at Grady and he smiled back.

"Yeah, maybe in New York..." Esme admitted.

"And you're decent at school, and swimming, and all those hours you spent on your stupid dance routines made you pretty good at ballet. That's what Dad says anyway."

"If you're trying to be nice, you're not doing very well."

"I'm your brother, I can't be TOO nice to you, it would ruin my reputation."

Across 14th Street, Union Square was bustling with people, many carrying bags of fresh produce from the farmers market on the far side of the square. As soon as they crossed the street, Scribbles started barking furiously.

"Here he goes, as promised," Esme said, pointing at two teenagers, a boy and a girl, skateboarding on the large, tiered plaza on the south side of the park. The sound of wheels scraping on stone as the girl did a power slide along the shallow step was enough to make Scribbles crazy. Esme scooped the dog up to try to calm him down.

"I know those guys from the Lower East Side skatepark. I'm gonna go say hi," Grady announced as he dropped his board to the ground and skated off. He glided up to the pair, then flicked his board up into his hand in one smooth motion while waving to the girl who was rocking cute white cut-off overalls. Then Grady fist-bumped the boy, a very short kid whose limbs were drowning in long baggy shorts and t-shirt. All three of them absentmindedly and adeptly fiddled around with their boards on the ground as they talked, as if the skateboards were extensions of their bodies.

"Scribbles, shhhh, no more barking," Esme coaxed, petting his head. But it wasn't helping at all.

"Esme, come here!" Grady yelled and motioned for her to join them.

"But he's going to freak out even more," Esme objected, looking at the girl effortlessly flipping her board around with her feet.

"I have an idea, trust me. Guys, hold up for a minute."

Everyone kicked their boards up and held them. Esme walked over hesitantly. No wheels moving, so no barking. This was an improvement, but Scribbles was still on high alert.

"This is Grace, and that's Jose," Grady said, pointing at the two other skaters. "This is my little sister."

"Hi. I do have a name. I'm Esme, and this maniac is Scribbles," Esme introduced herself and then turned to Grady. "What's your big idea?"

"What if we showed Scribbles that wheels are not the enemy?" Grady suggested. "Teach an old dog a new trick?"

"I don't know..." Esme was doubtful.

"We won't know if we don't try," Grady insisted. He sat down on the stone step and gently put his board down on the ground in front of him, being careful not to make any offending wheel noises.

"Bring him over here. Hey, Scribbles, good boy..." Grady reached out to scratch Scribbles' head as Esme sat down next to him, Scribbles in her arms. "You have treats, right?"

"In the side pocket of my backpack," Esme said. "I never leave home without them."

Grady fished the bag of treats out of Esme's backpack and shook them in front of Scribbles. He wagged his tail and panted at the sight, sound, and smell of the treats.

"Not so fast, Scribbles," Grady said, and looked at Esme. "Let's give this a shot. Put him on the skateboard, but hold on to him tight, so he feels secure."

Esme looked at Grady in disbelief. "No way. He'll go nuts."

"C'mon, worst case scenario, he starts barking again."

"It'll be cute!" Grace encouraged.

"Esme. What are you so scared of? Just try it," Grady insisted.

Very carefully, Esme lowered Scribbles onto the skateboard while Grady held the treats a few inches in front of Scribbles' twitching nose.

"Good boy, Scribs. I've got you..." Esme said soothingly.

"You're okay, want a treat, Scribbles?" Grady asked, crouching down in front of him, "Okay Es, start pushing him toward me. Sloooowly..."

Esme pushed so gently the skateboard seemed like it was in slow motion. Her body tensed in anticipation of an explosion of barking, but it didn't come. Grady backed away slowly, keeping the treats just out of reach. Esme held on tightly, slightly increasing the speed. They both kept the encouraging words flowing as they inched away from Grace and Jose.

"Shhhhhh..." Grady held his finger up to his lips and quickly backed up about ten feet. No more words, just the sound of the wheels. Grady shook the bag of treats as Esme continued toward him, pushing the skateboard with a hungry, but *quiet,* Scribbles on board.

"Good boy, Scribbles!" Esme and Grady exclaimed together as they crossed the imaginary finish line of their journey. Grady rewarded Scribbles with treats and they both crouched down for some congratulatory head scratches. Grace and Jose joined them, laughing.

"That was hilarious," Jose said. "It was like a military operation."

"That was amazing," Esme said. "His hatred of wheels is legendary! Julie and Poppy are never going to believe this."

"I got video!" Grace announced, holding up her phone. "And it was super cute."

"Awesome," Grady said, "text it to me."

"I'm so proud of you, Scribs!" Esme cooed as Scribbles' tail wagged like crazy. "Are you proud of yourself?"

"I think distracting him with praise and treats is the key, but you'll probably have to keep working on it. That barking seems like it is a pretty ingrained behavior," Grady said.

"That's for sure," Esme agreed, "but I'm psyched to tell Poppy and keep trying. We might have to borrow your skateboard."

"Um, you might have to come up with another plan. Sorry, sis, no one borrows my skateboard."

Esme stuck her tongue out at Grady again.

"Fine. We'll figure something out."

"Yeah, you will," Grady agreed. "And see what happens when you're not scared? Sometimes good things happen."

Esme realized immediately what he was talking about. She didn't need to be so scared. Something good might happen when they moved. Or when they started their new schools. Or joined new teams. But before she could respond, he jumped on his skateboard and pushed off in the direction of the farmers market.

"Last one there has to carry all the groceries home!" Grady yelled as he sped away.

"Wait, that's not fair! You have a skateboard! I have the dog! And you're bigger! And..." Esme shouted in protest.

Grady stopped short and turned around.

"Come on, Dismay. I'm just teasing. I'll carry the groceries," Grady said. "But let's go, I don't have all day to hang out with you."

Grady smiled at his little sister, and she ran to catch up with him. Maybe going to Union Square together wasn't the worst thing in the world. And maybe going to California together wouldn't be either.

CHAPTER SEVEN
Poop Patrol

Despite the muggy July heat, Chunky and Scribbles happily romped in the middle of the dog park, scrambling around a tennis ball with Madeline and Thor.

The girls sat, begrudgingly, on the only empty bench in the dog park—the bench closest to the entrance, which was also, unfortunately, the bench closest to the trash cans. The trash cans in the dog park were there for one reason only, and in the summer heat, they became dog poop ovens.

On the other side of the park, Suzanne stood with her arms crossed, shaking her head and carefully observing the playful crew. After a couple of minutes, she marched toward The Peonies, who sat up straight on the bench as she approached them.

"Does Liz know you're letting Chunky play with the big dogs?" Suzanne demanded. "She always told me it frightened her."

"Oh, yes, of course, Suzanne," Esme sputtered. "We explained how Chunky seemed almost sad being isolated from his friends in the little dog area."

"Liz said we have good judgment and she trusts us," Poppy added, nervously adjusting Precious in her lap.

"Hm. Well, French bulldogs are a tough little breed. He is certainly holding his own with Thor and Madeline, and they're practically three times his size. And I suppose it makes your job easier," Suzanne conceded, never taking her eyes off the pack of dogs and their tennis ball.

"It really does, and it sure looks like Chunky is happier, too," Esme said.

"Well, be sure to keep a close eye on him; you can't be too careful." Suzanne turned and marched back to her patrol position.

The girls looked at each other, sighed with relief, and turned back to observe the group of dogs getting a major workout as Precious sat watching from the sidelines, her head tilting back and forth as she followed the ball with her eyes. Precious didn't love being hot or getting dirty.

Thanks to the business cards they handed out on July 4th, Poppy and Esme also had two last-minute customers for the day: Tony and Elaine's new puppies. Meatball and Macaroni were chasing each other playfully nearby. An extra four dollars was always a good thing. And even though the puppies had a lot of energy, they were no problem for The Peonies. Unlike Chunky, who was presenting a bit of a problem.

"The smell from the trash cans is truly disgusting, Poppy. Can we go?"

"I wish. But Chunky is too busy playing to do his business. We can't take him home until he poops. With the babies, Liz already has enough poop to deal with!"

"Maybe we could borrow a diaper from the twins?"

They giggled at the thought of a French bulldog in a diaper, but their laughter was silenced as a gross odor filled their nostrils. They held their breath.

"Oh no, here we go again." Esme cringed as a woman opened a trash can to make a deposit. This released a wave of horrendous stench, and everyone with any experience knew not to inhale until it passed. Flies, like guards protecting their castle, buzzed furiously around the cans.

Poppy finally exhaled and exclaimed, "That's it. This is too much. We can't MAKE him poop."

"Yeah, and this smell is enough to MAKE me barf! C'mon guys, let's go!" Esme stood up and shook the leashes to beckon the dogs.

Chunky looked over and trotted toward the girls, and even Meatball and Macaroni came running. But Scribbles ignored Esme's call and continued his game with the big dogs.

"You too, Scribs. Let's go. Now!"

Scribbles reluctantly joined his crew and allowed Esme to fasten his leash.

They headed toward home with Precious, knowing the relief of air conditioning was waiting, leading the way. By the handball courts, a group of older boys was working out, doing push-ups, squats, and lunges.

"Look, it's Nico," Esme whispered as she looked down at Chunky, Meatball, and Macaroni.

"Just keep walking. He didn't see us." Poppy knew how shy Esme got around Nico. He was talented and nice, and she didn't blame Esme for having a crush on him.

The girls picked up the pace as they got nearer to the boys, kept their eyes dead ahead, and focused on their destination.

But Nico had seen them. "Hey, Esme. Hey, Poppy. You guys late for something?"

Poppy glanced at Esme, whose pale skin had already turned bright red, especially her ears.

"Oh, hi, Nico," Poppy said. "We're just rushing to get the dogs home; it's too hot out here for them."

"Yeah, it's brutal, isn't it?" he agreed, brushing his sweaty hair off of his face.

Poppy could feel how uncomfortable Esme was, and replied, "We really need to go. Come on Precious, Scribbles, everyone. Let's go."

Meatball and Macaroni obediently started to follow Poppy's lead. Esme tugged on Chunky's leash and stammered, "Come. On."

But Chunky dug in his paws. He wasn't budging.

"Chunk, come," Esme coaxed. Chunky was very well-trained and had never disobeyed Esme.

But he refused. He just stood there.

“Chunky. COME,” Esme commanded, with the biggest voice she could muster given the circumstances.

But the dog stayed put, staring at Esme.

“Chunky. NOW. COME.” She reached into her pocket for a dog biscuit, a last resort.

Chunky didn’t even acknowledge the treat.

“This is not like him,” Poppy said.

“Can I help?” Nico asked, “I can take these two and you can carry Chunky?” He reached for Meatball and Macaroni’s leashes. Esme glanced at him gratefully and squatted down next to Chunky.

“Come on, Chunk. We’re going home,” Esme said. “I don’t know why you’re being so stubborn.”

“Maybe he likes the heat. Maybe he wants to play more. Maybe he’s being a rebellious teenager,” Nico listed the possibilities. “Maybe he...”

Just then, Chunky decided it was the perfect time and place for a giant poop. An outrageously giant poop—something you’d expect from a Great Dane or a Mastiff, not a little Frenchie. Right in front of Nico, not to mention all of the other boys as well.

“Wow!” Nico said, his brown eyes opening wide. “Man, that’s a lot of poop for a little dog. Glad I’m not in charge.”

And with that, The Peonies realized THEY were in charge and looked at each other in horror. Picking up dog poop wasn’t the most glamorous part of the job, but they were used to it. Lots of biodegradable baggies and hand sanitizer. It really wasn’t that bad. But they weren’t used to having an audience.

Poppy, always the professional, moved into action, swiftly bagging her hand and then the poop in one quick motion. She knotted the top of the baggie while Esme stayed frozen in one spot.

"No biggie. Just part of the job. Totally natural—everyone poops," Poppy said matter of factly. She wasn't one to let emotions get in the way of doing her job.

Esme stared at Poppy, thankful that her normally subdued best friend was stepping into the spotlight for a change.

"You guys are total pros." Nico handed the leashes back to Esme, who blinked at him in disbelief—he wasn't grossed out, and he wasn't teasing them. He was actually complimenting them. Maybe there wasn't anything to be embarrassed about.

"Thanks, Nico," Esme said, finally breaking her silence. "No poop is too big for Peony's Prancing Pups!"

Poppy smiled. There was the Esme she knew and loved. Chunky started barking and grunting and pulling his leash toward home.

"Oh, NOW you're ready? See you later, Nico. Our work here is done," Esme stated with newly found confidence.

Nico laughed as the girls headed out of the park.

As soon as they were out of his earshot, they burst into laughter.

"Really, Esme? 'No poop is too big'? You've said barely one word in front of Nico since the play, and that's how you break your silence?"

"You started it! 'Everyone poops'? Gosh, I almost died."

"But you didn't. And neither did I. We are total pros."

"And Nico is even cooler than I thought," Esme added with a smile.

With all of the dogs safely returned, Poppy and Esme stood in the hallway outside Sir Charles' apartment. Knowing their time together was getting shorter every day, they hated to say goodbye.

"Want to hang out until my dad comes to get me for dinner?" Poppy asked.

"Totally!" Esme pushed open the stairwell door and the two started downstairs. "I didn't even know he was in town."

Will had been spending a lot of time at the beach taking pictures.

"Neither did I. It was pretty last minute. He had to come in for a gallery meeting or something."

"Where are you going?" Esme asked. Will loved good food and sometimes took Poppy to really cool places he'd read about online or in the Times.

"Patty's Buns. This will be our fourth time in a row."

"For good reason. That place is great!" Esme dragged her hand against the familiar worn plaster wall of the stairwell. "How many times do you think I've walked up and down these stairs?"

Esme had started thinking more and more about the move to California and the things that would be different. Like, her Grandma Marty's house in Los Angeles only had one floor. She never had to worry about dragging the laundry all the way up the stairs if the elevator was broken or there was a power outage. She could sit on her porch and actually look at the garden, not just the tops of buildings and a few random trees. And she could lounge in the pool and hear Grandma Marty chattering away through the kitchen window. But living in a house would never be as cool as living in an apartment building with her best friend.

Poppy's voice interrupted Esme's thoughts.

"Hmmm...We're eleven years old but we were in strollers for the first couple of years. So, taking the stairs for about nine years. Nine years times 365 days in a year is around 3,000 days. Add a few hundred trips when we were up and down the stairs more than once a day." Poppy tilted her head to one side as she considered her calculations. "I'd guess maybe 3,500 trips?"

Esme wondered how many floors her new school would have as they crossed the hallway.

Poppy pushed open the door to her apartment and switched on the ceiling fan.

"Crank up the AC," Esme demanded. "I think I have heat stroke!"

"You are always so dramatic." Poppy laughed, clicking on the air conditioning unit in the window. "I should change shirts before my dad gets here." She disappeared into her bedroom.

"Can I use your mom's laptop while you get ready?" Esme asked, glancing around the room for Sasha's computer.

"Hey, let's check out your new school!" Poppy yelled from her room. "I need to be able to picture exactly where you are every day, and I have no idea what you're getting into out there."

Kay and Sam had tried to get Esme to look at her new school's website with them a week earlier, but she didn't want to. Seeing it would make the move even more real, and Esme wasn't ready for that, or to act enthusiastic, or even interested. But if Poppy was interested, maybe it wasn't such a bad idea. And maybe it wouldn't be so scary if they did it together.

"Are you sure? I've been afraid to look."

Poppy came out of her room with a fresh t-shirt and a curious look on her face. "Why? Maybe we'll find something you can look forward to."

"Maybe. But I don't want you to feel bad if there is something for me to be excited about in California," Esme explained.

"I'd feel bad if you DIDN'T have anything to be excited about! Of course, it makes me sad to think about you being so far away and in a different school, but..."

"That's why I didn't want to talk about it with you. I don't want you to be sad."

"But we always talk about everything, Es," Poppy reasoned, "and we need to be prepared."

Esme smiled, relieved. Poppy always wanted to have a plan.

They sat down at the breakfast bar. Esme opened the laptop and typed in "0507," which was her own birthday and Sasha's code for everything. Kay's code for everything was "0424," Poppy's birthday. The moms thought they were being sneaky. But anyone who knew them could have guessed their password twist pretty easily.

Esme quickly typed the name of her new middle school into the search bar.

MEDIA CITY MIDDLE SCHOOL.

There it was. There was a big logo in the middle of the homepage with the words, "Media City Middle School, Home of the Palominos," surrounded by pictures of happy kids hanging out in the sunshine. She clicked on GALLERY to see more photos. The school wasn't just one building. It was a series of low, flat buildings surrounding a central courtyard with tons of outdoor space. And it seemed like the kids were walking between the buildings outside instead of through halls. It looked completely different from any school they had ever seen in New York.

Esme used arrows to click through the photos. They saw a bunch of kids wearing shorts and Vans, eating lunch outside on red picnic tables in the bright sunshine.

"You know what? I don't think it's ever rained a single time on any of our trips to see my grandma," Esme said.

"Never?" Poppy exclaimed. "I wonder if they ever have classes outdoors. That would be pretty cool."

Esme clicked again and there was a massive pool surrounded by kids in matching bathing suits and swim caps. A pool at school! Esme was a great swimmer and really fast because she was so tall and coordinated. She and Poppy had grown up swimming in the public pool in the park, which could get pretty crowded on hot New York City summer days. She couldn't imagine having a pool at her grandma's *and* at school.

"I feel bad for these poor kids." Poppy pointed at the screen. "They don't know what's about to hit the West Coast. I think you could beat any of these swimmers. Keep clicking."

The girls huddled over the computer, working their way through the website. They checked out the bell schedule (Esme would get out of a school a little before three, which would be almost dinnertime for Poppy), hot lunch menu (similar to the one at Poppy's new middle school, but with more avocado), and the activities (seventh graders took a trip to Washington DC every year!).

"Oh my goodness! What is that?" Poppy shrieked pointing to the screen and a brown cartoon horse with a white stripe down his nose and a big cowboy hat.

Esme leaned in and read from the screen. "'Yippee Ki-Yay! Git Along Little Dogies! Join Trigger at the

Midsummer Reading Rodeo!' What the heck is a Trigger?"

"Well, Little Dogie," Poppy said, throwing her arm around Esme, "I think you're going to find out soon enough. And I'm really glad we did a little research. There are some really cool things in California."

"I guess the pool is pretty cool," Esme conceded.

"And you won't have any stairs to drag your backpack up and down. And the outdoor cafeteria is like having a picnic every day!"

"All that's fine, but what if no one talks to me?"

"Well, we'll still have each other," Poppy reassured her best friend. "I'm going to a whole new school, too, so we're going to have a lot to discuss."

"We can email every day, right? From school or home."

"Or both! And you know our moms are going to be talking all the time, too, so we can hijack their phones."

"Maybe we can make a phone call schedule," Esme said hopefully.

"Totally, just like we do with the dogs," Poppy said. "And we've never missed a walk."

"That's true." Esme nodded. "Let's promise never to miss a talk either."

"Deal. Peonies forever."

"Peonies forever," Esme agreed.

CHAPTER EIGHT

In the Wink of an Eye

"This way," Esme commanded, haphazardly barreling toward the stage, narrowly missing picnic blankets that were already peppering the big lawn in Tompkins Square Park. The tote bag she was carrying swung dangerously close to people's heads as she moved. "We need to get a good spot."

"Es, there's plenty of space!" Poppy replied, carefully following Esme and smiling apologetically at the people as they passed. She clutched a colorful tapestry under each arm. "And the concert doesn't start for half an hour."

"At the pace they're moving, they'll miss the whole thing," Esme exaggerated, gesturing at Kay, Sasha, and Sam, who trailed behind them casually.

Eventually, she said, "Phew, this is perfect." Esme stopped in a shady spot with her feet wide apart to claim her turf and waved her long arms wildly at the parents, who were engrossed in conversation. "Poppy, quick with the blankets, we have to save room for Julie, too."

"Calm down, Es," Poppy said, shaking out the tapestries in the light breeze. Esme guided them as they floated to the ground over the lush grass, designating their area. She plopped her tote and herself down and started unpacking.

"Hmmmm...let's see what we have. Pasta salad, half a bag of pita chips, hummus, olives, some baby carrots, and baba ganoush. Ew. Grady and I didn't like it. I guess Mom is hoping one of you guys does!"

"Baba ganoush is eggplant dip, right?" Poppy inquired, and Esme nodded. "I'll try it. My mom bought a rotisserie chicken and a loaf of that good bread from the Corner Café."

They didn't overplan on nights like this, everyone just brought whatever they had on hand or something easy to grab in the neighborhood to share and hoped for the best. It usually worked out just fine, but if not, their favorite ice cream parlor, Rainbow Sprinkles, was right across the street.

"Nice spot, Peonies!" Sam said as he approached the girls and looked around. "Great view of the stage."

Sasha handed a canvas tote filled with snacks to Poppy.

"Unpack that please, Pop. Oooh, yummy! Baba ganoush!" Sasha said as she sat down next to Poppy. Poppy winked at Esme, who grimaced and wrinkled her nose.

"Tell that to my ungrateful kids," Kay teased, giving Esme a fake glare. "Oh, there are Julie and Suzanne. Hey guys, over here!"

"And Suzanne's sister is visiting from New Jersey," Sasha said, popping a pita bite piled with baba ganoush in her mouth and waving. Julie awkwardly waved back, struggling with a cooler in one hand and Scribbles' and Madeline's leashes in the other. Julie and Suzanne were on the far side of the stage, accompanied by a third woman who looked almost exactly like Suzanne, but who was extremely, extremely pregnant. Suzanne held her sister's arm protectively, carefully guiding her toward the group.

"Hey, everyone," Julie said as she approached. Scribbles and Madeline tugged at their leashes as soon as they saw The Peonies. Or as soon as they smelled the chicken. Probably a combination of the two.

"Hi, pups! Hi, Julie!" Poppy and Esme greeted the dogs by scratching their heads. Julie handed over the leashes to Esme while Poppy put her body in between the dogs and the food. Madeline had her favorite big bone clenched in her strong jaws.

"Hi, Suzanne. And you must be Joan," Sam said. "I'm Sam. Here, let me help you." Joan looked pretty uncomfortable as Sam and Suzanne carefully lowered her to the ground. Suzanne actually looked a little uncomfortable, too. She wasn't used to being out of her element in the dog park.

"Are you okay, Joanie? Be careful, Sam!" Suzanne commanded.

"Geez, I'm pregnant and a little uncoordinated, but I'm not made of glass!" Joan laughed. She looked around and smiled at the group. Suzanne pulled a small pillow from her backpack and placed it gently against her sister's lower back to make sure she was comfortable.

Julie took a seat and pointed at Kay. "Joan, this is Kay, Sasha, and..."

"Obviously, you two are The Peonies," Joan interrupted. "I've heard a lot about you both."

"Nice to meet you," Poppy said, extending her hand formally. She was surprised that Suzanne had told her sister about them. She never paid that much attention to them unless she suspected them of doing something wrong.

"Hi!" Esme just waved and held up the leashes. The dogs had settled down; Scribbles was tucked in between Madeline's front legs, pressed up against her powerful chest. Madeline closed her eyes immediately.

"She's beat. We just came from a long playdate with Thor and Tab," Suzanne explained, unfolding a small blanket and trying to drape it around Joan's shoulders.

"Geez, sis, I'm fine. It's the middle of July! You don't need to fuss over me." Joan tossed the blanket toward Poppy, who caught it in one hand. "Good catch!"

The feast grew as Julie retrieved a big container of sliced watermelon, corn and black bean salad, and a bag of tortilla chips out of the cooler. Sasha carved the roast chicken and Kay peeled plastic wrap off the pasta salad. Sam stretched out his long legs, tucked Kay's now-empty tote bag under his head like a pillow, and closed his eyes.

"This looks great," Joan said, admiring the meal. "Thanks for having me. I'm trying to get out as much as I can before..." She patted her belly.

"When are you due?" Kay asked.

"I'm close! Next month!" Joan answered excitedly. "And Auntie Suzanne is going to come out to New Jersey to help me for a few days. Oh, speaking of which..."

Joan struggled to turn around and tried to reach for Suzanne's backpack.

"Oh, please let me. Don't push yourself," Suzanne chastised as she reached into her backpack and pulled out a clear shoebox-sized container with something wrapped in foil inside.

Esme leaned over and whispered in Poppy's ear, "It's weird to see Suzanne be so caring about someone who doesn't have four legs and a tail."

"Esme, stop." Poppy giggled, even though she knew she shouldn't.

"Special delivery from my favorite place in New Jersey. Two dozen sliders. Since I got pregnant, they're literally all I want to eat," Joan said enthusiastically, peeling back the foil.

Scribbles' head popped up as a delicious smell wafted out of the foil. Madeline's nose wiggled a little, but she stayed asleep.

"Wow, she really is beat if that smell doesn't wake her up!" Esme laughed, leaning over to peek in at a pile of tiny burgers with onions and cheese on fluffy white buns.

"Hand one over," Sam demanded, without even opening his eyes.

Esme reached in and distributed the mini burgers to the group.

"Check, check. Check one, two, three." A voice boomed through the speakers across the park, startling everyone.

A woman tapped the main microphone center stage to check the sound while a few other technicians hustled around, setting up. Two techs adjusted the speakers on the side of the stage and another carried some cymbals to the drum kit.

"You know, there have been some really important events here in Tompkins over the years," Sam said knowingly. He really was like an encyclopedia sometimes. "The Grateful Dead even played here once!"

Julie, Suzanne, and Joan nodded, confirming this fact. They had all grown up together in the neighborhood and knew its history.

Poppy leaned over to Esme and asked, "Who are the Grateful Dead?"

"An old band from California," Esme whispered. "My dad's obsessed."

"I know it was before your time, but do you know anyone who was there?" Sam inquired eagerly.

"Actually, our parents were," Suzanne said tentatively. She wasn't used to being in the spotlight anywhere but the dog park.

"Really?" Sam sounded impressed.

"Oh, they wouldn't have missed it. They were both writers and activists in the counterculture movement in the 1960s," Joan explained, popping a slider in her mouth.

"'Counterculture movement'?" Esme repeated.

Joan nodded, her mouth full, gesturing for Suzanne to continue.

"The counterculture movement had a lot to do with young people challenging the 'old fashioned' ideas of the 1950s. They believed in equal rights and free speech for all people, protecting the environment for future generations, things like that..."

The girls nodded; this was all stuff they believed in, too.

Suzanne continued, sounding more and more authoritative, like she usually did.

"There was a lot of art, literature, and music created to express these new ideas. And lots of gatherings in Tompkins to share them."

"I'm actually named after Joan Baez, the singer and civil rights activist," Joan chimed in.

"Wow, that's cool," Sam said. "I wanted to name Esme 'Pigpen' after the guy in the Grateful Dead, but Kay vetoed the idea."

"And for that, I will always owe you, Mother," Esme said dramatically.

Poppy, on behalf of her friend, swatted Sam playfully with Joan's rejected little blanket.

"And all these years later, people are still coming to Tompkins for live music!" Julie interjected, and as if on cue, the band started playing.

Five musicians filled the air with soothing instrumental jazz music. The drums and upright bass created a meditative rhythm while the saxophone, clarinet, and piano took turns improvising solos. Poppy looked around at their extended friend-family who had all settled into their spots. Sam continued to lounge with his eyes closed on the far edge of the blanket, with Kay and Sasha sitting next to him. Esme was now lying down next to Poppy with her eyes closed, just like her dad, with the dogs' leashes lightly hooked over her foot. The dogs were behind the girls—Scribbles on patrol, watching all of the people around them, and Madeline passed out, sleeping with her bone under her foot like a teddy bear. To her left, Julie, Suzanne, and Joan all swayed to the music. Poppy smiled at how much Esme looked like Sam and how much Suzanne looked like Joan. Genetics were cool.

"Hey everyone, eat up!" Julie said. "We don't want to have to drag all this home."

"I'll take another one of those sliders," Sam said, holding out his hand. "You don't have to ask me twice."

"Me too," Esme said.

"Me three," Suzanne and Joan said at the same time as they both raised their hands.

Julie laughed and handed out the sliders, and everyone continued to pick away at their dinner while they listened to the music. Poppy slipped Scribbles a bit of chicken, but only a tiny bit. She knew people food could make dogs sick if they ate too much or if it was too different from their regular diet. But Scribbles wanted more. He trotted over to Poppy and jumped in her lap. He licked her hand and wagged his little tail, trying to butter her up with his cuteness. She patted his unruly curls and giggled to herself; they really did have similar hair. But twins or not, she wasn't going to succumb to his manipulative ways. He (and Julie) would thank her later when he didn't have a tummy ache!

"Wink! Wink, come back!" a woman's voice rang out behind them.

Poppy turned to see where the interruption was coming from. She didn't see the woman, but she did see a tiny, tan, one-eyed Chihuahua running toward them at top speed. The dog stopped short just a couple of feet from their blanket. The hair on the back of his neck stood straight up, and his lone eye locked on Madeline's bone.

Scribbles stood up; his tail tensed. The two dogs were around the same size. The other dog took a step toward them. Scribbles barked twice, but Madeline didn't wake up.

"It's okay, Scribbles," Poppy said quietly, trying to calm him.

The Chihuahua took another step forward, his single eye flicking back and forth between Scribbles and the bone. He growled low and long, flattened his ears, and showed his pointy little teeth. Scribbles barked again.

Then, like a flash of lighting, it happened.

The other dog lunged for the bone, and Scribbles leaped out of Poppy's lap, his leash slipping off Esme's foot as he charged the dog.

"Scribbles, no!" Poppy yelled.

But it was too late. The other dog was desperate for that bone and wasn't about to let anyone get in its way. He turned and snapped his teeth at Scribbles, growling furiously. Scribbles started to bark and growl back. Poppy jumped to her feet, and the grown-ups and Esme all turned around. Even Madeline finally woke up. But before anyone even had time to register what was happening, Poppy looked around her and grabbed Joan's discarded blanket.

She threw it over the Chihuahua just as he was about to clamp his teeth into Scribbles' neck. Then she kneeled down on the edges of the blanket and held it firmly as the dog frantically tried to get out, snapping at the blanket from inside.

Julie snatched up Scribbles, Suzanne grabbed Madeline's collar, and Esme held tight to Madeline's leash. A woman came running toward them.

"I'm sorry! Did he hurt anyone? Is he okay?" She was frantic. The Chihuahua calmed down a little when he heard the woman's voice.

"No, everyone is okay," Poppy said, her voice a little shaky.

The woman knelt next to Poppy and started to pet the dog through the blanket, softly whispering to him.

"It's okay, Wink. You're okay, shhhhhh…just calm

down. It's all right, I have him." Poppy stood up slowly and the woman carefully picked up Wink, still swaddled in the blanket. Sasha put her arm around Poppy.

"I'm so sorry," she continued, "I'm Donna, I'm fostering him. He's had a very rough life. He was the victim of dog fights in the past. That's how he lost his eye."

"That might explain why he wasn't afraid of Madeline," Suzanne said quietly. "He's probably had to defend himself from bigger dogs before."

"Maybe the concert was too much, too soon. He literally jumped out of my arms," Donna continued, still gently stroking Wink's quivering body. She looked at Poppy with gratitude and handed her the blanket. "Thank you."

"You're welcome," Poppy said. "I really hope he'll be okay."

"We're working on it. Have a great night," she said and walked away, holding Wink.

The group crowded around Poppy.

"Wow, Pop! You were like a superhero. That was amazing!" Esme threw her arms around Poppy. "You seriously saved the day."

"It happened so fast," Poppy said, "I didn't even have time to think, I just had to...do."

"How DID you know what to do?" Suzanne asked.

"The internet," Poppy replied quickly. "We did tons of research when we decided to start the business. It would have been irresponsible not to and expect people to trust us with their dogs."

"That's my partner," Esme declared proudly. "Always prepared."

"I knew there were a few ways to stop a dog fight by distracting them—"

"Water works. But there's no water around to throw on them here," Esme chimed in.

"Right. And no air horn handy," Poppy continued.

"I don't know if that would have helped with the band playing," Esme reasoned. "They might not even have heard it."

"So, my next option was to throw a blanket over the dog so he couldn't see Scribbles anymore," Poppy concluded.

"I'm very impressed, girls," Suzanne said genuinely, nodding her approval. "That was quick thinking, really skillful canine handling, and well, I'm very grateful you stopped the fight before Miss Lazy Bones Madeline woke up. That could have been a disaster. She would have instinctively defended Scribbles AND her bone."

The girls looked at each other in shock. Suzanne was actually complimenting them. She actually thought they did a good job. She was actually *impressed*.

"Yes, great job, Poppy," Sam said, tousling her hair.

"I'm so proud of you, Peanut!"

"Me too," Kay agreed.

"Me three. Hey, do I get any credit for not wanting that blanket in the first place?"

Everyone turned around to look down at Joan, who was still sitting in exactly the same position she'd been in all night, legs awkwardly crossed with her hands resting on her bulging belly.

"I totally would have helped, but I couldn't get up by myself!" she joked. "You all just left me down here all alone with the last few sliders."

"Well, why don't we join you down there and enjoy the rest of the concert?" Sam said, resuming his spot. "That was enough action for one night! I'm as exhausted as Madeline!"

Everyone laughed and sat down. Esme reached for a couple of slices of watermelon, handed one to Poppy, and whispered, "We might see some more dog walking action, now that we have Suzanne's approval. Who knows what might happen?"

"Who knows?" Poppy replied, spitting watermelon seeds onto the grass. "But the seeds have been planted!"

CHAPTER NINE

the trouble with Zipper

As soon as the girls got to the third floor to pick up Precious, they were surprised by spirited voices, hearty laughter, and upbeat, old-fashioned swing music. Everyone tried to keep pretty quiet on Sir Charles' floor, especially now, when he was recovering from his knee surgery. But as they got closer, they realized the sounds were actually coming from *inside* Sir Charles' apartment. They looked at each other, bewildered.

"What's happening?" Esme whispered. "What's going on in there?"

"Shhh..." Poppy shushed her and held her hand up to her ear, gesturing for her to just listen.

The clanging of metal rang through the hall as they approached the door.

"I told you to be careful! That's my favorite copper skillet!" Sir Charles' voice came into focus. The words were firm, but his tone was downright jolly.

“Oh relax, Charlie, I promise this brunch will be worth it!” replied a low, friendly voice, followed by unfamiliar barking. “Tab, quiet! Back away from the bacon.”

Poppy turned to Esme and mouthed, “I think it’s Todd, from the dog park.”

“Only one way to find out,” Esme whispered back and knocked on the door, firmly enough to be heard over the racket.

Poppy was right. Moments later, the door swung open, and there was Todd, with Tab underfoot. He was wearing khaki shorts, another Hawaiian print shirt, and the same pink clogs he had been wearing the day Poppy met him. However, he was also wearing a very crisp cotton apron with the British flag on it, which he had clearly borrowed from Sir Charles’ pristine kitchen. Todd’s hands were covered with flour, and his face was dotted with little beads of sweat.

“Well, hello,” Todd said, looking down at the girls, “nice to see you outside of the dog park!”

“Hi, Todd,” Poppy replied, “We’ve come to get Precious for her walk.”

“Hello, girls,” Sir Charles called from the couch behind Todd. One leg was propped up on the ottoman, his knee in a heavy black brace. Precious sat delicately on his lap. She was freshly groomed; her silky, brown-and-white fur was trimmed into a very short summer haircut, and rainbow ribbons adorned two tufts of hair by her ears. "I'd forgotten you'd already met Todd, Poppy. He's an excellent, but very untidy, chef."

"Is that really the thanks I get?" Todd asked. "You'll change your tune after you eat!"

"It does smell divine," Poppy said, using one of Sir Charles' favorite words.

"Divine, indeed!" Todd agreed, opening the door wider and gesturing for the girls to come in. "I made quiche lorraine–with farm fresh eggs, a homemade crust, of course, and overflowing with cheese and bacon. And a mixed green salad with my secret vinaigrette dressing. And a pint of Charlie's favorite dulce de leche from Rainbow Sprinkles for dessert!"

The girls glanced over at the kitchen. 'Untidy' was an understatement, it was an absolute disaster. It seemed like every bowl and utensil Sir Charles owned had been used and left out on the counter; scraps of vegetables were scattered on the floor; and there was flour everywhere. It was a good thing Sir Charles couldn't see the mess from his seat on the couch. Esme raised her eyebrows at Poppy, who smiled. Thankfully, they weren't the ones who had to clean it up.

"Todd knows I'm simply razzing him," Sir Charles said. "I am deeply appreciative of all of his caretaking while I've been rehabilitating."

"At your service," Todd replied, gently bowing in Sir Charles' direction, who rolled his eyes at being teased back. "And this kitchen is so much bigger than mine, more room for me to spread my culinary wings." Todd winked at the girls and then turned to his dog. "Tab! Out of the kitchen! No more bacon for you."

Tab barked hungrily and stared up at Todd, waiting.

"Think you girls could handle an extra dog?" Todd asked. "I don't think he'll let us eat in peace as long as he can smell bacon!"

Tab barked again, as if he understood the word 'bacon.'

"Absolutely!" Esme said. "It's always fun to have a new dog in the crew."

"Wonderful. Let Charlie enjoy a little quiet time." He nodded toward the kitchen and whispered, "Plus, I have quite a bit of cleaning up to do. Shhhh..."

"Come on, Tab. Let's go for a walk!" Poppy said. "You too, Precious."

"How much do I owe you?" Todd asked, reaching into his pocket. "I think I have some cash..."

"Don't be silly, Todd, allow me," Sir Charles interrupted. "Peonies, why don't you just put it on my...Tab."

Todd groaned at the corny joke, but he was grinning broadly at Sir Charles. The girls were stunned by Sir Charles' out-of-character behavior and were trying hard not to show it. They rushed toward the door with both dogs, anxious to discuss this curious situation.

"Well, we should be on our way," Esme stammered, "but we'll be back soon."

"But don't worry, not too soon," Poppy added. "Enjoy your quiche!"

"Oh, we will," Sir Charles said. "As I said earlier, Todd is an eggs-ellent chef!"

Esme and all the dogs waited impatiently on the library steps as Poppy returned some books. The early-August heat was blistering so their walk had been shorter than usual. But Poppy insisted they stop. She would brave any weather to return library books on time.

Esme looked down at Chunky, Scribbles, and Tab, who were panting like crazy. Meanwhile Precious seemed comfortable thanks to her newly-shorn coat.

"What a fancy hair-do you have, Precious," Esme said, fiddling with the two rainbow ribbons on Precious' head. "Maybe I should cut my hair, too. It might be a little cooler!"

Esme's long blonde hair was in two bundles, too, two braids decorated with shiny silver bobble elastics at the ends. Even so, her Peony's Prancing Pups t-shirt stuck to her skin as the sweat poured down her back.

Poppy finally emerged from the library. "Come on Esme, let's roll. Time to get these pups home."

The posse headed home, fortified with vitamin D from the sunshine. They got to Lucky Stars and saw Julie through the window, head down, magnifying glasses on, soldering iron in hand, focused squarely on a piece of jewelry in the vice attached to her bench.

Scribbles naturally veered toward the door of Lucky Stars, but Poppy noticed the daily specials on the sandwich board outside the Corner Café and pulled him right past the shop.

"Oooh, Esme, check it out! Today's special iced tea is passionfruit! That's by far the best one! Can you treat? Please? I'll hold the pups."

"Geez, I have to get them AND pay? That doesn't seem fair..." Esme teased her friend.

Poppy rolled her eyes, plopped down on the bench outside Corner Café, and wrapped the four leashes around the arm of the bench. All the dogs somehow wormed their way into the shady spot under the bench where Zachary, the manager, always left a bowl of fresh, cool water for the neighborhood dogs. Precious promptly fell asleep.

Poppy noticed a young dad pushing a stroller toward them, humming softly to his smiling baby.

"Easy, Scribbles," Poppy said as she sensed him tensing up at the sound of the approaching wheels. "No barking, it's okay."

The Peonies had been paying lots of attention to rewarding Scribbles' improving behavior since the skateboard experiment. Scribbles let out a single yip as the stroller passed, and then looked up at Poppy expectantly.

"Good boy! Almost...we'll keep working," she stealthily slipped him a treat. A few moments later, all four dogs were napping happily under the bench. Poppy was gazing down the street, daydreaming about her delicious, organic, caffeine-free tea, when she felt a tap on her shoulder.

Poppy turned around quickly to see a young man with a hipster billy-goat beard and wide smile, staring at her inquisitively from under the brim of a huge straw hat.

"I'm Milo, from the East Village Update, the blog about the neighborhood. I've noticed you and your friend in the park. Nice shirts, by the way!" Milo waved through the café window at Zachary, who waved back enthusiastically from behind the counter and gave him a thumbs up.

Milo took off his hat and a tumble of dreadlocks fell out.

"Oh, I know you! I didn't recognize you without seeing your dreads!"

"Most people don't," Milo laughed. "I don't even know if my mom would recognize me without them. Hey, I would love to talk to you guys about your business. I think it would be a great story for the blog."

Esme burst through the door carrying two iced teas, which were already sweating in the heat.

"Milo, meet my best friend and business partner, Esme."

"Super great to meet you," said Esme. "Zachary told me you're a reporter. That's awesome. Our families always read the East Village Update. I wonder if they have anything like it in California? 'Cause I'm moving at the end of the summer. Which is so LAME."

"ESME." Poppy put her hand over Esme's mouth. "Milo wants to write a story about us. But you need to chill!"

Esme nodded her head, confirming that she would

chill, and Poppy slowly removed her hand from Esme's overactive mouth.

"Sorry, I get a little excited sometimes."

"No worries," Milo reassured her. "Like Poppy said, I'm here to listen. I'd love to hear all about your business." Milo took a little green notebook from one of what seemed like a hundred pockets in his colorful patchwork backpack. "So, I think I got the beginning...you're moving?" He peered at Esme.

The girls looked at each other and sighed heavily. They explained the circumstances to Milo, who nodded as he followed along and took notes.

"So, the bottom line is you girls took kind of a bummer situation and turned it around to make sure you had a great summer together AND got a really special token of your friendship. That's a pretty inspiring story."

"Thanks, Milo. It's definitely better than moping around and counting down the days until I move."

"That's for sure," Poppy agreed. "Now we're mostly just counting how much more we have to raise before we can buy the peony necklaces! We're getting there."

"Really impressive, girls. And I think you could have even more business after the article comes out!"

Poppy and Esme high-fived each other, when out of nowhere, Zipper, the Wu's bodega cat, snuck up to Precious and swatted the napping dog right on the nose. Precious suddenly leaped up and into action unlike anything they'd ever seen. Zipper took off like a shot, her collar bells jingling, headed for the safety of home. Still sound asleep, Chunky, Scribbles, and Tab didn't even notice when Precious pulled her leash right out of the loose knot around the bench.

"Precious!!" both girls yelled as the dog chased Zipper toward the bodega. For a fourteen-year-old who hated the heat, Precious was moving like a champion husky in a dogsled race!

"Go, go!" said Milo. "I'll watch these guys!" He gestured to the other dogs.

The girls bolted after Precious, both imagining what Sir Charles would do if anything happened to his precious princess. Mrs. Wu stood outside the bodega, where she had been misting the vegetables with her hose. Zipper darted around her owner and through the open door, and Precious uncharacteristically ignored the spray of water to stay right on her tail.

"Get out of there! Precious! You can't be in there!" Mrs. Wu shouted, the hose spraying water everywhere as she waved her arms frantically.

The girls ran through the spray just as Zipper raced across a display of five-gallon buckets filled with fresh flowers. The shelving unit wobbled precariously. Zipper bolted up a ladder at the back of the store to a high ledge. She was safe, but as Precious turned the corner to continue the chase, she spotted the precocious cat on her perch and lunged.

Poppy and Esme watched in disbelief as Precious

knocked into the flower display and it began to topple over. Buckets of water and flowers dumped all over the floor.

Mrs. Wu ran into the store, still holding the streaming hose.

"Oh no!" she yelled, adding even more water to the flood on the floor. "This is a disaaaaaassssssssssst–"

And just as she spoke, Mrs. Wu slipped on the slick, wet floor, her feet flying out from under her. Like a baseball player sliding into home plate, she shot toward another shelf and sent a display of peanut butter, jelly, maple syrup, and honey crashing to the ground.

Poppy and Esme stood as still as statues as Precious, her new hair style totally ruined, began to lick peanut butter off the linoleum. Mrs. Wu sat in a puddle of water, daisies, and jelly, but didn't appear to be hurt. She was just soaking wet, and still holding the running hose.

Milo and the other dogs appeared in the bodega doorway and stared at the mess.

"Mrs. Wu? Girls? Is everyone okay?" Milo asked nervously.

No one said a word. Precious daintily picked her way through the debris toward Mrs. Wu. The tiny spaniel lay down in a bed of grape jelly, put her head on Mrs. Wu's lap, and helped herself to a smear of honey from her dress for dessert.

Mrs. Wu's face crinkled up like she was about to cry, but instead, she started to laugh, which made Milo laugh, and eventually, Poppy and Esme started to laugh, too.

Esme began to pick up the spilled flowers and put them back in the buckets, being careful to avoid broken glass. Milo grabbed the mop and bucket from behind the counter and pitched in, his dreadlocks swinging from side to side as he mopped.

Poppy helped Mrs. Wu to her feet, grabbed Precious and the hose, still running, and walked outside. Together, they rinsed the peanut butter and jelly, maple syrup, and honey out of Precious' fur.

"It looked worse than it really was," Milo said, joining them outside. "Only two peanut butters, three jelly jars, and one honey bear actually broke."

"I think most of it ended up on Precious," Mrs. Wu said. "And the flowers were mostly fine."

"We just lost a few blossoms," Esme added. "The peonies weren't even spilled!"

"The Peonies always seem to be okay," Mrs. Wu joked. "Honestly, I haven't laughed that hard in ages, and the hose was a welcome break from the heat. Let's just not tell Mr. Wu about any of this. He would not be amused."

"Oh no," Poppy said, holding up the two flat, limp rainbow ribbons she'd removed from Precious' hairdo. "These are ruined!"

Esme reached up to her own hair and pulled off the silver bobbles securing her braids and said, "These will work. And they'll match any outfit Sir Charles is wearing—metallic goes with everything."

The girls both turned to Milo, mop still in his hand.

"Listen, Milo..." Poppy said tentatively, "about the article. I'm hoping you don't need to report ALL the details you saw today?"

"I don't know what you're talking about. All I saw was two hard-working girls and a few happy dogs." Milo winked and tucked his dreads back into his hat. "Keep your eyes on the blog. The article will be out in the next couple of days." He walked away, whistling.

"We're really sorry, Mrs. Wu," Esme said, restyling Precious' hairdo with her own silver bobbles. "It was an accident."

"It's okay. Accidents happen. And it only took a few minutes to clean up with everyone's help."

Poppy focused intently for a moment and then reached into her fanny pack and pulled out some money. She glanced at Esme, who nodded in silent agreement.

"I think $30 should cover the lost merchandise. We're really sorry," Poppy reiterated, handing the money to Mrs. Wu.

"Apology accepted, and thank you," Mrs. Wu said, taking a single ten-dollar bill from Poppy's hand. "This is plenty. I'm guessing Zipper had more than a little to do with it. She's such a tease."

And as if on cue, Zipper zipped out the front door, probably off to find another unsuspecting, sleeping dog.

CHAPTER TEN

A toast with toast

Sasha and Poppy sat peacefully at the breakfast counter, enjoying fresh summer blueberries from the farmers market. A pair of mourning doves were gently cooing to each other on the windowsill, when suddenly, their quiet morning was interrupted by a loud, insistent banging on the door.

Poppy sat upright on her stool.

"What the heck?" Sasha wondered aloud as she made her way to the door. She looked through the peephole and said, "Oh, for Pete's sake...Take it easy, Esme!"

The door was barely open a crack when Esme shoved her way into the apartment past Sasha.

"It's up! It's up! The story on the blog...! Come on, come on...come upstairs...Everyone's waiting so we can read it together!" Esme demanded, tugging on Sasha's leopard print adult onesie. Even in the summer, Sasha wore footie pajamas to bed—she didn't like bathrobes and said onesies made her feel cozy.

"Seriously? Mama, come!" Poppy did a familiar little dance in place. It was sort of a funky version of the Hokey Pokey the girls had been doing since their Mommy and Me music class when they were toddlers. Poppy shook her left hand, her right one, kicked each foot out to the side, and then wiggled her butt while she shimmied her shoulders.

"Yeah, Sasha, come!" Esme smiled at Poppy and joined her. The girls now moved in sync, perfectly choreographed.

"All right, all right...Stop giving me commands. I'm not one of your dog clients. I need a second."

Sasha grabbed her coffee mug from the counter and followed. The two families were together so much, their dishes were always going back and forth between apartments. They ended up back in the right house eventually.

Sasha locked the door behind them, laughed, and started dancing. She knew the moves, too, and the girls' energy was contagious. They continued dancing and laughing all the way up the stairs to the sixth floor.

As they got to apartment 6B, Sam swung open the door, recognized what was happening, and joined in, shaking his booty in his favorite "Kiss the Cook" apron like his life depended on it. Everyone laughed; even Grady cracked a smile.

"Get in here!" Sam motioned them in with his whisk. "Anyone for some scrambled eggs with a side of famous kids?"

Everyone started filling their plates with scrambled

eggs, bacon, and toast. Sam wasn't always great at family dinner, but he was the master of scrambled eggs.

"Dad, c'mon, we're not famous yet!" Esme protested as she spread grape jelly on her toast.

"Kay, will you do the honors?" Sam asked, passing his laptop to Kay.

"Happy to," she replied and pulled her reading glasses out of the pocket of her painter's smock. Both chic and practical, Kay's smocks had become part of her official uniform, even when she was teaching, shopping, or just hanging out.

Kay began to read.

Everything's Coming Up Peonies for Local Business

East Village eleven-year-olds Esme and Poppy, took a personal situation that was for the dogs and turned it into a bed of roses, or rather, peonies.

The two best friends, known throughout the neighborhood as "The Peonies," were devastated to learn that Esme's family would be moving to California at the end of the summer.

"Instead of moping around, we decided to make it the best summer ever," explained young entrepreneur Esme.

With the goal of purchasing real rose gold friendship necklaces designed by local Lucky Stars shopkeeper, Julie, the two girls looked for an opportunity to earn money, have fun, and spend time together. They found the perfect solution right there in Lucky Stars—right under their feet, in fact, in shop dog Scribbles.

Poppy explained, "Julie needed to focus on her work and her customers, and Scribbles needed to exercise and be walked. And we knew she wasn't the only one who needed help with their dog."

Looks like these girls were barking up the right tree. With a whole litter of happy clients, The Peonies are well on their way to bringing home those necklaces!

Everyone burst into applause.

"Amazing, girls! And the picture is terrific!" Kay said as she turned the laptop to face the group.

The vibrant colored photo *was* terrific. It was taken from behind, showing off the PPP logos on their t-shirts perfectly. The girls' heads were turned to look at each other, their huge grins in profile, and the bright blue sky behind them highlighted their contrasting hair colors. At their feet were their three primary clients, all obediently looking up at them with love.

"Where'd this photo come from, Peanut?" Sasha wondered, using her favorite pet name for Poppy. "Usually it's your dad who takes the pictures around here."

"Milo must have taken it before he even introduced himself. Before you went into the café for iced tea, Es."

"That's what I call investigative reporting. I didn't even notice! It is a great shot."

Sasha's cell phone began to ring. "Honestly, it's like he can hear us talking about him...I think Will has ESP sometimes. Pop, it's your dad."

"Hey, Daddy! Did you see?" Poppy asked, taking the phone and putting him on speaker.

"Totally! What a great article, baby."

"Your kid's a star, Will!" Sam yelled toward the phone.

"Oh, hey everyone. Can I join you? Any breakfast left?"

Before anyone could answer, there was a knock on the door and it opened. There was Will, grinning mischievously, his unruly jet-black curls looked like he had just stepped out of a wind tunnel. A camera hung around his neck as always, and he held a box of donut holes.

"Krispy Kreme, anyone?" he offered as Poppy jumped into his free arm. "I stopped down at 2B first and then figured you guys were up here."

"2B or not 2B, that is the question. Am I right?" Poppy joked. They had studied William Shakespeare's plays in school last year.

"An oldie but a goodie, Poppy. Hey, Will." Sam went in for a fist bump with his old friend. "Long time no see."

"Hi, Will," Sasha greeted her ex, kissing him on his dark brown, freckled cheek. "You look well-rested." Even though Sasha and Will weren't a romantic couple anymore, they still cared about each other a lot. Sasha always told Poppy how good it made her feel to see Will looking healthy and happy. Since she and Will both loved Poppy so much, Sasha wouldn't want it any other way.

"It's the slow pace and ocean air," Will said with a smile, "but I'm getting a lot of work done, too."

"I saw some of the rough images on your Instagram,"

Kay said. "I can see why the shore inspires you."

"What's up, G-Dog?" Will asked as he handed the donuts to Grady. "What are you now, like seven feet tall?"

Grady took the box, stood up, and looked down a couple of inches at Will. "Seven and a half, actually."

Will laughed. Like his father, Grady liked to joke around. And Will was an adult who appreciated Grady's sense of humor and didn't mind being teased a little.

"We need to toast the girls!" Sam announced. "Everyone grab a slice."

He held up a slice of toast like a glass of fine champagne; everyone followed suit.

"I'd like to propose a literal toast to The Peonies in honor of your hard work, your entrepreneurship, and your friendship. Girls, I know I speak for everyone here when I say we are so proud of you both. Real rock stars. Congratulations!"

"Here, here," everyone said, pretending to clink their toast together.

Everyone sat down, and Poppy snuggled in next to her dad. Esme smiled at seeing Poppy so happy. It was great having Will there. They all really loved each other. It was like one big family, not two little ones. Esme knew how lucky she was to get to see her dad every day and sometimes took it for granted. Poppy didn't mention it much, but she missed her dad, especially when he was away for big chunks of time. Esme bet Will missed Poppy, too.

The idea of missing Poppy hit Esme like a punch in the gut. There were less than two weeks left in the summer, less than two weeks until she moved away, less than two weeks until *she* would be the one missing Poppy. Every. Single. Day. She tried to push the thought from her mind quickly. But her eyes welled up with tears.

She quickly wiped them away before anyone noticed. This was a celebration, and she wanted to keep it that way. She could think about moving later.

"The Peonies forever!" Esme said, holding her toast toward Poppy.

Poppy smooshed her toast against Esme's as if they were making a blood pact. Esme's grape jelly got in her butter, but she didn't even mind.

"Yup," Poppy replied earnestly, "Peonies forever!"

CHAPTER ELEVEN

Dog Run 911

"It's weird being on the street this early," Poppy commented as The Peonies raced toward Tompkins Square Park.

Sam had received an urgent call, a pup emergency that sent the girls out much earlier than usual. The sun was up, but most of the neighborhood shops weren't even open yet. Corner Café had a few early customers sitting at tables, sipping coffee and nibbling on pastries. But that was it. The only other light the girls saw was coming from the kitchen of Drew's Diner, but even his sign still said Closed.

"We should get cinnamon rolls on the way back," Esme suggested. Not even an emergency could kill her appetite.

"What exactly did your dad say?" Poppy asked, more concerned about the next few minutes than their next meal.

"Just that Suzanne needs our help at the park."

The idea that Suzanne would ask for help in the first place was strange, but it was even stranger that she'd ask for theirs. She always treated them like little kids instead of practically middle schoolers. Maybe seeing how they handled Wink at the concert, and then Milo's article, had changed her mind.

When Poppy and Esme arrived, they spotted Suzanne and Madeline standing in the small dog run, which was odd because Madeline was definitely not a small dog. As they approached, Suzanne pulled her phone away from her ear.

"Oh good. Thanks for coming. Just give me a minute." She was all business as usual. Then she pointed to the fence and added, "There's a hole," before walking off to continue her call.

The girls looked at each other, puzzled, then looked at the fence, which was actually more like two fences tied together. One was black wrought iron and made the park look fancy. The second was practical chain link and kept the dogs inside. A big section of chain link had come loose, leaving an opening about eight inches wide. Not huge. But definitely big enough for a small dog to wiggle through.

"Is that the emergency?" Esme wondered. Surely there were plenty of people in the neighborhood more qualified to fix a fence.

"I don't know," Poppy said. "But the morning crowd is going to be here soon. Let's see what we've got."

Not knowing what awaited them at the park, Poppy had filled her backpack with supplies before she left home. When she dumped the contents out on the grass, about thirty loose dog biscuits fell out, along with two tennis balls, three granola bars, a spare leash, some hand sanitizer, a roll of poop bags, a notebook, and assorted colored pens.

Esme held up a treat, "We could try distracting the dogs..."

Poppy smiled. It was a creative idea but not a permanent solution. She fished out the spare leash, "Could we use this to tie it back together?"

Esme wasn't convinced but shrugged anyway. "We can try."

"Well, now that that's taken care of," Suzanne was walking back toward them with Madeline following close behind, when she stopped in her tracks. "What on earth are you girls doing?" She looked confused.

"Helping?" Poppy responded weakly, gesturing to the fence.

"Oh! You thought that was my emergency? No. I found it that way when I got here. I reported it to the Parks Department and I just hung up with Todd. He offered to secure it after his breakfast."

Just then, Madeline, who had been by Suzanne's side, picked up a tennis ball and dropped it at Poppy's feet. Poppy looked at Suzanne for permission.

"Go ahead."

Poppy threw the ball as hard as she could, and they all watched as the muscular dog raced quickly after it.

"She's the reason I called."

The girls knew how much Suzanne loved Madeline, so they straightened up and paid extra close attention.

"The Peonies reporting for duty." Esme gave an exaggerated military salute. "What's up?"

"Joan's baby is coming early, like *now*."

The girls didn't understand what that had to do with them, or with Madeline, so they just waited for Suzanne to explain.

"I've got to get on a train to New Jersey ASAP, but Hound Hotel doesn't open until nine. So I need you guys to watch Maddy until they open, then walk her over there and drop her off. They know her and I've already left a message."

Poppy and Esme were stunned. Suzanne was going to trust them with her beloved best friend. This was a pretty big day for Peony's Prancing Pups.

"Us? Are you sure?" asked Esme.

"Yes, I am. I think you'll do fine..."

The girls smiled.

"And honestly, nobody else could get here as quickly."

Knowing that made it a little less special. But it was still pretty exciting. Then it hit Poppy. Hound Hotel was all the way up on 14th Street.

"But..."

"I know," Suzanne stopped her. "It's a little outside of your approved walking zone, right?"

Poppy nodded.

"I explained the situation to Sam, and he said it was

okay as long as you call him when you get there and then go straight home."

Wow! It was a big day.

"You can count on us," Poppy promised.

"I'm sure I can."

Madeline ran up with the ball and dropped it for Suzanne. The park was starting to fill up, so Poppy re-stuffed her backpack and they all headed over to the big dog section. Suzanne called out to the other puppy parents as they went, warning them about the fence.

Suzanne noticed the main poop bag dispenser was empty, took a fresh roll out of her purse, and inserted it. Then she opened her wallet and looked in.

"Hmmm. I don't have any singles. Can I pay you the two dollars when I get back?"

The Peonies looked at each other and silently agreed. Suzanne did so much for the park, they couldn't take her money.

"That's okay. This one's on us," Poppy said.

Suzanne looked back inside her wallet, pulled out a ten-dollar bill, and said, "I tell you what. If you guys will keep your eye on the park while I'm gone—just make sure the fountain drain stays clear, put any lost toys in the lost and found, and scoop up any poops that get left behind, I'll pay you ten dollars."

"Deal!" Esme grabbed the bill from Suzanne's hand. "We can do that."

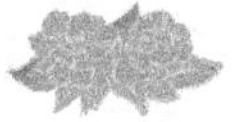

It was almost time to take Madeline to Hound Hotel and pick up their regular canine customers for the morning walk, but Poppy and Esme had decided to wait for Todd to arrive and fix the fence. Suzanne had left them in charge. They planned to take that responsibility seriously.

"Did somebody order a handyman?" Todd was carrying a bright orange toolbox. Tab trotted happily along at his side, carrying the end of his own leash in his mouth.

"Hi, Todd!" the girls called out. "Hi, Tab!"

At the sound of his name, Tab dropped his leash and ran up to the bench. He sniffed and licked the girls enthusiastically, then dove for Poppy's still unzipped backpack, snatched it up in his mouth, and ran off.

The girls jumped up, but Tab was too fast. He was already across the park, running in circles, open backpack in his mouth, treats flying everywhere. Thor came out of nowhere to check out the action, and suddenly, four big dogs, including Thor and Madeline, were chasing after Tab, eating up the biscuits as they fell to the ground.

Esme ran after him, but Poppy knew not to bother. Todd would call him back.

"Well, looks like he's the one being herded for a change," Todd said with a smile.

Then he put two fingers in his mouth and whistled loudly. Tab, Madeline, Thor, and a tan and white puppy called Frances all came running toward them. Esme came up behind them with the backpack in her hand. Her face was red, and she was out of breath. Poppy was worried she might be a little bit mad that nobody had helped her chase after Tab. But she just dropped the backpack on the bench, turned to Todd, and asked, "Do you think you can show us how to do that?"

Madeline was a well-behaved dog and had been playing all morning, so the walk over to Hound Hotel was easy. That is, until they were a few doors away. Then, her long, ropey tail started wagging furiously as she put all of her fifty pounds of muscle into straining against the leash—*toward* their destination.

"Wow!" Esme said, grabbing the leash with both hands. "And I was worried she'd be sad about being boarded."

The girls hustled to keep up.

"Me too," Poppy said, pulling the tall glass door open for Esme and Madeline.

The girls had passed by Hound Hotel with their parents many times, but they'd never been inside. It was pretty fancy, and they were kind of surprised that Suzanne sent Madeline there instead of leaving her with a friend, like Julie.

As they walked in, to their right was a small area with

dog toys and upscale treats for sale. To the left was a gated area in front of a window with fluffy dog beds. Straight ahead was a check-in desk, just like at a fancy people hotel.

Behind the counter stood a woman wearing a crisp, white button-down work shirt with a blue Hound Hotel logo on the pocket. She was short and about their mothers' age, with long dark hair pulled back with a pink bandana. She looked up and saw them.

"MADDY!"

Madeline pulled with all her might toward the friendly woman.

"You can let go," the woman assured them. Then she held up a treat and in a commanding voice told Maddy to sit. The big dog ran up, stopped right in front of the desk, and sat down. The woman deftly flicked a dog treat over the counter, which Madeline caught just by opening her mouth.

"You must be The Peonies," she smiled at them warmly.

Poppy was a little embarrassed when Esme did her goofy salute again and announced, "That's us. I'm Esme, and this is Poppy, and we're—"

"Peony's Prancing Pups. I can see that," the woman pointed at their shirts. "Also, I read the East Village Update." She rang a little bell on the counter, then continued. "Very impressive. I'm Rosa, and I'm Hound Hotel."

The girls looked around. Behind the counter was a big open area with more dog beds and toys, and at the back were swinging doors to what they imagined must be where the dogs slept. It was clean and organized and very professional.

A teenage girl wearing the same shirt as Rosa appeared through the swinging door.

"Madeline's here. Give her a bath and then let her take a nap before playtime."

"Yes, Rosa," the girl stepped out from behind the counter and took Madeline's leash. She patted the dog's head, and Madeline happily went with her.

"Wow." Esme couldn't help herself. "This place is so cool."

"And it's all yours?" Poppy asked.

"Sure is. I started this business out of my apartment ten years ago and built it up into the chicest dog hotel and grooming service in all of New York City," Rosa waved her hand and twirled around behind the counter.

The girls were awestruck. Rosa was successful and confident but also fun and casual, just like they hoped to be.

"Suzanne said to make sure you call home," Rosa pointed to the phone.

In all of the excitement of the morning, they'd completely forgotten. Esme picked it up and dialed.

"Would you like to sign Madeline in?" Rosa turned a big book with blank lines around. Poppy filled in the spaces for the dog's name and owner's name, then started to look in her backpack for her notebook where she had Suzanne's phone number.

"Don't worry about that." Rosa filled in Suzanne's

number from memory. "Maddy's a regular customer. She's been staying with me since the apartment days."

Poppy thought to herself, *That made sense*. Suzanne *was* leaving Madeline with a friend. Her friend just happened to own the chicest dog hotel in New York City.

Esme hung up the phone and it was time to go. They said goodbye to Rosa and rushed out the door. They had their own regular customers to take care of and they didn't want to be late.

CHAPTER TWELVE

Rainbow Sprinkles

"Shhhh...! Girls, please keep it down," Ms. Borden shushed Esme and Poppy for the third time.

"Sorry, Ms. Borden," Poppy apologized from their favorite table in the back corner of the East Village branch of the New York Public Library.

Ms. Borden was smart as a whip, as kind as could be, and had an uncanny way of knowing which books The Peonies would love. Sometimes she set aside new books for the girls the minute they arrived at the library. Other times, she recommended classics that made Sasha and Kay smile with nostalgia. But as great as she was, Ms. Borden also took her position very seriously. She did not tolerate excessive noise in her library, even from two of her star cardholders.

"I don't see what the big deal is," Esme whispered, glancing around the empty library. "We're the only ones here!"

It was blissfully peaceful at the library—if people

weren't out of town on vacation, they were at Rockaway Beach, Coney Island, or at the Hamilton Fish public pool on the Lower East Side. Added bonus: the air conditioning was always blasting in the library.

"Keep counting!" Esme yell-whispered as Poppy organized dollar bills into stacks of ten. There were eleven fives, nine tens, and four twenties already tucked away in a pink Lucky Stars envelope.

Poppy counted aloud quietly as she came to the end of her pile of cash, "Six, seven, eight, plus these six piles of ten. That's sixty-eight dollars."

"Plus the $225 in the envelope," Esme reminded her.

Poppy concentrated as she added in her head. "Grand total…$293."

"OMG!" Esme whooped and jumped to her feet. "We're so close!"

"ESME!" Ms. Borden looked up. "Don't make me have to ask you to leave."

Esme ran over to the front desk.

"I'm sorry, Ms. Borden. But it's such great news…" Esme looked at her expectantly.

"Okay." Ms. Borden folded her hands on her desk and gave Esme her full attention. "Tell me all about it. But please keep the volume down."

Esme took a deep breath and straightened up as if preparing to deliver an important speech.

"You see, we, Poppy and I, The Peonies, celebrity dog walkers and proprietors of Peony's Prancing Pups, are very, very close to our goal of $350. Enough to buy our very, very special friendship necklaces. In fact, we have a mere...umm...well..."

Esme turned to Poppy for help.

"A mere fifty-seven dollars left to earn," Poppy chimed in, rescuing her friend from doing math under pressure.

"Great work, girls. That's very impressive. But you're not going to earn fifty-seven dollars sitting in the library being shushed by me. I'm trying to shop for new YA books for fall, and I need to concentrate," She looked up at the clock on the wall behind her. "Maybe you girls could wrap it up and give me some peace and quiet?"

Now, it was Poppy's turn to yell, as she looked up at the clock and noticed the time.

"I've got to go, Es. I am totally late for jujitsu. Take the money..." she said, thrusting the bulging envelope into Esme's hand and running to the door. "I'll catch up with you later!" she called, her words trailing off.

Esme tucked the envelope into the back pocket of her jeans and bounced toward the exit.

Out in the sunshine, Esme patted the envelope in her pocket. They were so close! Then she made a spur-of-the-moment decision. Instead of heading home, she turned right, drawn like a magnet to Rainbow Sprinkles Ice Cream on the other side of the park.

Poppy would definitely understand the need to celebrate! Esme thought to herself, and she was right. They always agreed on ice cream.

A singsong voice greeted Esme as she pushed open the heavy glass door covered with rainbow and unicorn stickers.

"Welcome to Rainbow Sprinkles! How can I make your day? Tell me what flavor you're feeling. 'Cause then for sure, that's what I'm dealing!"

Esme laughed, paused, and rapped back awkwardly, "Hey there, Jimmy! You are way too kind, but give me a minute to make up my mind!"

"Good one, kiddo. You're getting better," Jimmy encouraged her. "Where's your other half?"

"She's at jujitsu, I'm on my own for a little while today until my dance class," Esme explained, peering at the chalkboard that listed all the fantastic flavors. "Oooh, you've got some new combinations."

"Take your time, take it all in," Jimmy sang, gesturing at the sign with a grand sweep of his arm, ending with a sharp snap. "I've got the greatest creations, the sugary sins."

As Esme's eyes scanned the menu, her mouth started to water uncontrollably at the choices. How could she decide? Would she get The Sunken Treasure (chocolate, marshmallow, and bananas sliced like gold coins), The Little Brother (mint chocolate chip, protein powder, and trail mix), The Iron Hand (vanilla, blueberries, and extra, extra, extra whipped cream), The Mama Bear (black raspberry, Swedish fish, and snickers), The Princess Poop (strawberry, strawberry sauce, gummy bears, glitter sprinkles), or The Andy's Candy (sour cherry with crushed Pez candies and licorice chunks)? They all looked amazing!

She was lost in the possibilities when a familiar voice startled her.

"You gonna take all day? Some of us have places to be!"

Esme spun around and was face to face with... Nico. Behind him stood a line of six people, all waiting impatiently for ice cream.

"Ummm, I'm sorry...it's just, so many, umm..." Esme stammered, but then collected herself. "You know, Nico, I just can't decide! What do you think? Is it a chocolate day or a fruity day?"

"I'm boring," Nico confessed, "I get the same thing every time, chocolate and vanilla twist in a plain cone with chocolate sprinkles."

"That's not boring." Esme said, turned confidently to Jimmy and ordered, "A Princess Poop for me, and the regular for the gentleman."

"Thanks, Es. I owe you one."

"No problem, business is good!" Esme said, pulling the envelope out of her pocket and handing Jimmy some bills.

"Wow, that's great! Congratulations!" Nico smiled at her. "I'm super impressed."

Nico was treating her like a friend, a *girl*...not just Grady's little sister. Esme felt like a million bucks and beamed with pride. She reached toward the counter as Jimmy presented the two delicacies.

"Here you go. Two frosty treats!"

"Thanks, Jimmy. I'll see you soon!" Esme handed the vanilla and chocolate twist cone to Nico and took a huge bite of Princess Poop.

"Have fun at dance class, and don't leave the other Peony out next time!" Jimmy laughed as he turned to the next customer.

Nico held the door for Esme. "Yeah, where is Poppy? I can't remember the last time I saw one of you alone."

Esme was devouring her ice cream, but came up for air to respond. "She's at jujitsu. I took a few lessons. It wasn't my thing, but Poppy's obsessed."

"Really? How come?" Nico asked.

"She loves all the rituals and rules. She likes how you measure your improvement with tests and stripes and belts. Poppy is really competitive! You should see her spar!"

"Wow, I would not have thought that. She seems so quiet."

"She seems quiet, but she's usually just focused or planning. She actually stopped taking dance to do jujitsu... it's kind of weird not being with her." Esme got quiet.

"I know how you feel." Nico's smile faded.

Esme hadn't thought about how he must be feeling.

"It's going to be so weird without Grady," he continued. "We're not like, The Peonies or anything, but..."

"You're best friends, too," Esme finished his thought.

"Yeah," he agreed. "High school without Grady is kinda hard to imagine." Then he shrugged his shoulders, took a big lick of ice cream, and smiled.

Ice cream cures everything, Esme thought, *at least for a little while.*

"It'll be okay," he continued. "We'll both make new friends. People like us are irresistible."

"You think so?" Esme's stomach fluttered. Was he telling her she was irresistible?

"Sure. You'll make plenty of friends at dance class in LA."

"Oh, man, speaking of dance class, I've got to run," Esme stopped in front of a trash can, took her last bite of ice cream, and threw away her empty cup and spoon. "This is my last one in New York after six years. I don't want to be late!"

"Well, thanks for the ice cream. Hope I can treat you before you move!"

"It's a date!" Esme said without thinking. She waved and turned toward her house. She barely had time to make it home to change.

"OMG, OMG, OMG!" Esme muttered to herself as she ran. "WHY DID I SAY THAT? 'IT'S A DATE'?? I'm going to die."

Esme replayed the scene over and over in her head as she changed into her tights and leotard and dashed off to dance class. She couldn't wait to tell Poppy all about it. But that would have to wait.

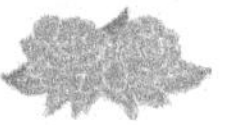

Exactly seventy-two minutes later, Esme burst into Poppy's bedroom breathlessly, sweating and still buzzing, "Poppy, you will not believe what happened after you left. I mean, it was totally bonkers. Nico! Nico! Nico!"

"Whoa Esme, calm down! I can't even understand you! You're acting insane," Poppy laughed.

Esme took a deep breath and started over, "I had a full-blown, practically grown-up interaction with...NICO."

"Wait, what?" Poppy stared at Esme. "Nico? You didn't... like, kiss him or something, did you?"

"OMG, no! But we talked, and we walked. And OMG, he's so cute. And I wasn't even really nervous. And he's funny. And he was being sensitive. And he likes soft serve twist with chocolate sprinkles. And I think he thought—that I thought—that he asked me out on a date. OMG. I can't believe I did that..." Esme was spinning out of control again.

"Tell me every single detail in order. Let's go up to your place so you can change. We can get a snack and go through this calmly."

Even when it was a matter as urgent and important as Nico, Poppy liked things to be orderly and logical. And she didn't mind reviewing details multiple times.

Upstairs in 6B, Esme took a speedy shower while Poppy

helped herself to some snacks for their summit. They would need to be energized and nourished to properly analyze all of the details of the encounter with Nico.

Poppy settled cross-legged on the bed with a bowl of cucumber slices and cherry tomatoes, as Esme stretched out on the floor in front of her, still just wrapped in her towel. There was no time to waste getting dressed.

"Okay, spill it," Poppy said. "Spare no details."

Esme dramatically told Poppy about every single moment, in detail. Occasionally, Poppy would ask her to repeat something ("Wait, so he said you were 'irresistible'?"), or they would take a moment to explore the potential meaning behind Nico's actions (was it a coincidence that he was walking in the same direction as Esme, or did he just want to hang out more?).

Eventually, Poppy asked, "What made you decide to buy him an ice cream?"

"It just happened...I was feeling so proud and excited. I was holding our money and I just took a chance and ordered for him!"

"Well, I'm not thrilled about all of these unapproved expenses," Poppy teased, "but I am super proud of you for being so bold. I don't think I could have done that..." Then she glanced around the room. "Where is the money, anyway? Where are we keeping it?"

Esme was in such a rush getting ready for class, she hadn't put their money away. She rolled over and reached for her jeans, which she'd left in a puddle on her bedroom floor. She flipped them over, patted the back pockets—lightly at first, then frantically. Finally, she sat up, shaking them.

Poppy leaned forward and put her snack bowl on the desk next to the bed.

"Esme...please tell me you have the envelope."

"It's got to be here. It was right in my back pocket the whole time!" Esme shook her jeans again, and reached into the pockets over and over, as if that would make the envelope magically appear. But it was gone. Esme looked up at Poppy hopelessly, her eyes wide with disbelief and fear.

"Think, Esme, come on," Poppy pressured. "Where was the last place you had it?"

"I, I, well, I paid for the ice cream, and then I swear I put it right back in my pocket, but I..." Esme struggled to remember more details.

"This can't be happening." Poppy was in disbelief. She pushed Esme to think back, "Did you see anyone weird in Rainbow Sprinkles?"

Esme shook her head no.

"Did you sit down anywhere?" she pressed.

Not that Esme could remember.

"Which way did you walk?" Poppy's voice got louder and sterner with every question.

Esme stared at the floor and answered so softly Poppy could barely hear her, "I don't know. I can't remember..."

Poppy sat up very straight, clutching the edge of the

bed with her fingers, her shoulders raised and tense. Her eyes narrowed as she began to speak.

"We have worked all summer, and you just threw all that work away because you got distracted by a boy and were only thinking about yourself."

The words stung. Esme didn't look up. Filled with shame, she stared down at the floor, unable to meet Poppy's gaze.

Esme steadied herself and argued, "It was an accident. And you're the one who had to run off and leave me all alone to take care of the money. We should have put it somewhere safe together."

"Leave you alone? I was being responsible as always; I had to get to jujitsu on time."

"Well, you should have counted faster, then. If you're so responsible, maybe you should have managed your time better." Esme was grasping at straws.

"I can't believe you're trying to turn this around! YOU. LOST. IT." Poppy said each word slowly and deliberately.

Esme realized she didn't stand a chance. She DID lose the money, but she wasn't ready to back down. Poppy could be so smug sometimes.

"Sorry I'm not perfect all the time, like you," Esme spat, seething.

"Or like your perfect Nico? You were so engrossed by his perfection that you managed to lose all our money?" Poppy snapped back.

"Poppy, I didn't mean to lose it, and it wasn't Nico's fault either."

"Well, it sure wasn't MY fault, so whose fault was it?!" Poppy asked, her voice quivering with anger.

"It was my fault, and I'm sorry, Poppy...but...if you were in my shoes, you would have been distracted, too!" Esme protested.

"I can't believe how irresponsible you are. I always have to take care of everything. I never should have trusted you with our money!"

"But, Poppy, we trust each other with everything!"

"Maybe I shouldn't have." Poppy stood up. "Well, at least I won't have to worry about it once you move."

Esme stared at her, shocked, hurt, ashamed, but also angry—how could Poppy be so mad?? It was an accident!

Poppy opened the door to leave.

"Wait, Poppy, please! You're not being fair! Let's figure it out!" Esme pleaded, tears filling her eyes.

"There's nothing to figure out, Esme. We're done."

"Done?" Esme was furious now. "You're telling me that $293 is more important to you than our friendship? Really?"

"Actually, $293 minus whatever you spent on Nico!"

"Fine! Just go!"

"Fine! I will!" And with those words, Poppy stormed out the door.

CHAPTER THIRTEEN

A Delicious Distraction

Esme sat on the floor of her room, packing books and toys into cardboard boxes. She felt terrible. With only a little over a week left until the big move, she'd lost all of their money. Even worse, she'd lost her best friend. She could hear Kay calling her from the kitchen but was too upset to answer.

"Esmeralda?! Are you in there? Esmeraaaalda!"

"Yes, mom," she finally managed to mumble.

Kay knocked softly on the door. "I thought we were going to make those Cauldron Cakes for family dinner tomorrow?"

In trying to cheer Esme up about the move, Kay made a list of all of the fun things they were going to do in LA, including visiting The Wizarding World of Harry Potter at Universal Studios where the treats were sold.

"I bought all of the supplies."

Esme didn't feel like baking.

"Go ahead without me, mom."

"But you were so..."

"I'm not in the mood!" Esme snapped, cutting Kay off mid-sentence.

"I'm coming in," Kay announced and barged right in.

Esme looked up at her mom with puffy, red eyes. Kay sat down beside Esme on the floor.

"Oh, honey, I know this is hard."

Esme shook her head, sniffling. "You don't understand."

"I do. I'm going to miss our friend-family, too. And we're all so proud of you girls for everything you've done this summer..."

The knot of sadness and anxiety in Esme's chest exploded in one loud wail, followed by uncontrollable sobbing.

Kay put her arms around her daughter and held tight.

They sat like that until Esme caught her breath and wriggled free. "No, you really don't understand, Mom. I did something horrible."

She slowly explained all about the money and the ice cream and finding her pocket empty. She left out the part about Nico. It was just too embarrassing.

Kay nodded kindly but didn't say a word. When Esme was finally finished, she asked, "Have you told Poppy yet?"

Esme nodded.

"And...?"

"She hates me!!!" Esme yelled, falling back in her mother's arms.

"I'm sure she doesn't hate you," Kay objected. "She's upset. And understandably so, right? You guys worked really hard to earn that money."

Esme nodded again. She knew she had blown it.

"How much was it?" Kay asked.

"We had $293!"

"Wow." Kay's eyes went wide with surprise. "That much?"

"She's never going to forgive me," Esme added.

"How do you know? You've never had a fight like this before."

"That's how I know. We never really fight."

"There are disagreements and problems in every relationship, Esme."

"Not The Peonies. Not you and dad."

"Oh Esme, is that what you think? Arguments are normal, sweetie. Life can be tough sometimes. Difficult situations come up. What defines us, and our relationships, is how we handle them. I have faith you two will get through this. But right now, I need help in the kitchen, and I'm not going to take no for an answer."

Kay's little speech made no impression. Esme was still beside herself. "Do I have to?"

"Yes. You do." Kay grabbed Esme's hand and pulled her along, pretty sure that a creative, and yummy, project was just the distraction her daughter needed.

Kay put on "Cheek to Cheek," one of their favorite playlists to bake by. On it, Lady Gaga, who used to live close to their neighborhood before she got super famous, sings old-fashioned songs with a man named Tony Bennett. When Esme first heard it, she thought it was boring. But, as with everything, her mom made her give it a try, and the music grew on her.

Esme pouted at first, shuffling around the kitchen with her head down. But the music, and the project, quickly got the better of her. Before she knew it, she and Kay were swaying and dancing around the kitchen, organizing all of their delicious cauldron components. They lined up chocolate frosting, chocolate filling, and the chocolate cupcakes Kay had made earlier in the day. They melted chocolate chips, filled pastry bags, and followed each step carefully. Her mom was right. It was exactly the distraction Esme needed. Finally, Kay carefully pushed one of the little chocolate "handles" they'd made into the top of each cake while Esme followed behind, sprinkling white chocolate shavings, and voilà! Their Cauldron Cakes were done, and they looked amazing!

"That was easier than I expected," Kay smiled, admiring their handiwork. "But then again, I had an excellent assistant."

Esme felt pretty proud. She started packing one up to bring downstairs to show Poppy, like she did every time she and Kay made something special. Then she caught herself. Her smile disappeared and her shoulders drooped. She felt sad all over again.

"Hey, why don't you bring one of those to Julie tomorrow?" Kay encouraged. "She'd love that."

Esme knew it was a good suggestion. Julie dressed up like a witch pretty much every Halloween. But what if Poppy was there hanging out...?

Oh no!! The dogs!! What were they going to do about walking the dogs tomorrow? Neither of the girls had missed a single day of dog walking all summer.

Esme took her responsibilities very seriously, but she was going to have to call in sick. She just wasn't ready to face Poppy. Besides, Poppy was so mad she had probably already changed the name of their business to Poppy's Prancing Pups.

"Mom, I don't feel well. I don't think I can walk the dogs tomorrow."

"That was sudden." Kay put her hand on Esme's forehead. "You don't feel hot..."

"It's my stomach."

Kay suspected Esme was faking it but decided to let her off the hook. Maybe a day apart was all the girls needed.

"Well, if you aren't feeling well, probably best to stay in. I'll call Sasha and let her know. Why don't you go back to packing your room? Lie down if you feel really awful."

As Esme turned to go, she eyed the fudgy, decadent Cauldron Cakes. They had turned out great, and any other day she'd be excited to try one. But suddenly, thinking about Poppy, she was just too sick with sadness to imagine ever eating again.

CHAPTER FOURTEEN

the Mean Streets

Poppy walked solemnly down the street with Chunky and Precious, who were blissfully unaware of why Esme wasn't with them. They trotted along happily on their regular route to pick up Scribbles. Poppy had postponed the morning walk because of a massive summer thunderstorm, which also allowed her to mope around the house a little longer.

The storm had left the air thick and hot with moisture, and the ground was damp with little rivers of water trickling across the sidewalk. It was appropriate weather for Poppy's mood.

She pulled her baseball hat down over her eyes and pushed her sunglasses up tight to her face, hoping Tony wouldn't notice her from behind the pizza counter. It didn't work.

Tony's booming voice rang out of the pizza shop. "Hey, Peony, only half a bouquet today? Where's your partner?"

"She's sick, I guess. Just me today," Poppy yelled extra loudly to make sure he heard her the first time. She wasn't in the mood to get into a big discussion with Tony about Esme.

"Tell her I hope she feels better!"

"Who cares..." Poppy muttered to herself but gave Tony a phony enthusiastic thumbs up.

Zachary, who was writing the specials on the sign outside Corner Café, bent over to greet the dogs. He scratched all around Chunky's thick neck and gently patted Precious, whose silky-smooth coat was already growing back.

"Good afternoon, pups. Good afternoon, Pops." He smiled at the threesome. "No Esme? Who's gonna hold the dogs while you get your passionfruit fix?"

"She told her mom she had a 'summer cold'," Poppy said.

"Wow, what a bummer! She's moving soon, isn't she? What a terrible time for her to get sick!"

"Well, I'm going to have to get used to handling things on my own, so it's not the worst thing to get some practice."

"But you're going to miss out on some of your last days together. That's the bummer."

"Listen, Zachary...it's not a big deal. I don't have to do everything with Esme," Poppy snapped rudely.

"Yikes, sorry to pry. How about an iced tea? I have passionfruit," Zachary offered kindly.

"I'm fine. Sorry. Maybe I'm a little under the weather,

too…" Poppy fibbed. But she sure didn't feel like talking about Esme anymore!

Poppy gave the leashes a little yank. "C'mon guys, let's get Scribbles. Maybe I'll grab that tea later, Zachary."

Scrappy Scribbles started barking hello before Poppy even opened the door. Julie looked up and waved her in, smiling.

"Hey, girl! Where's Esme?"

"Esme is sick." She rolled her eyes. *Why is everyone always asking about Esme,* Poppy thought. "And I'm not sure how much longer we're even going to be in business."

"Ummm. Alien alert. What grumpy teenage life form has taken over your body? I'd better call Esme and tell her something is VERY wrong with her best friend."

"Why does everyone keep talking about Esme? I'm here. I'm keeping the business going. I've got everything under control. As always," Poppy snapped, again.

"Okay, Pops. You're clearly having a moment. I don't know what's bothering you, but maybe a walk will help you shake off this mood." Julie looked back down at her workbench, putting an end to the conversation.

Poppy suddenly felt embarrassed. She'd never been rude to Julie before. She walked toward the park with the dogs, kicking herself for letting her feelings about Esme cause her to treat other people poorly. There was no excuse.

Everything felt muted and dull in the park. As if she were in the middle of a thick cloud, Poppy barely noticed the squirrels running right in front of her, teasing the dogs, or the bed of rose-purple coneflowers that was in full bloom, or the jazz musicians assembled by the fountain playing a cheerful version of the old standard "When the Saints Come Marching In."

Any other day, Poppy would have been enchanted and delighted by each of these things, but today they seemed lackluster, and she just made a beeline for the dog run.

She looked around nervously, crossing her fingers that she could avoid the park regulars—she was afraid of how she might act and really didn't feel like explaining where Esme was. Again.

Luckily, the park was quiet. Poppy scooped Precious up in her arms to keep her feet clean and found a bench in the farthest corner.

She tried to think about anything other than Esme—her jujitsu test next week, organizing her closet by color, what was for dinner. Ugh. Dinner. It was family dinner night, and it was at her house. Esme was coming over. Surely they would cancel. Esme was "sick."

When Poppy returned to Lucky Stars, Julie was showing some colorful mobiles to a young couple with a stroller. She shyly waved and dropped the leash on the counter. Julie barely made eye contact with her, staying focused on her customers.

Poppy put her head down and practically ran back to the apartment building to drop off Chunky and Precious, doing her very best to avoid any more conversations. Her plan to go straight to her room was interrupted by Sasha, who was sitting at the table with her laptop and a mug of tea.

"Hey, Peanut, how was it out there?"

"I'm sick, Mom. I need to go lie down."

"Come here, let me feel your head..." Sasha insisted, reaching out her hand.

"It's not that kind of sick, Mom, it's my stomach...I feel like I'm going to barf. Maybe we should cancel family dinner," Poppy suggested, walking toward her mom.

"Well, we all have to eat and it's our night to host. I've got a chicken in the oven already." She pulled Poppy in closer. "Peanut, this doesn't, by any chance, have anything to do with the fight you and Esme had, does it?" Sasha asked gently.

"No, Mom, I'm just sick. I don't know what you're talking about," Poppy objected, but she knew her mom knew. Sasha and Kay must have talked about it.

"It won't help to keep it bottled up. Family dinner is happening—you guys had some space this morning, but I'm sure you will work it out."

"It's not that simple, Mom. And it doesn't matter anyway...Esme's leaving. After next week, who even cares?"

"You're right, it is complicated. Feelings always are. So, are you mad about the money? Or sad that Esme is moving? Because they're both valid, sweetie."

"Both, I guess, and I feel bad. I was really, really mean to

Esme. I actually wanted to hurt her feelings. I'm ashamed about that. Am I a mean person?" Poppy felt like she was going to cry just thinking about it.

"Sometimes even the nicest people do mean things when they're upset. Listen, Esme didn't mean to lose the money, and you didn't mean to hurt her."

"Then why do I still feel like I'm going to barf, Mom? I don't think I can face her..."

Sasha looked at the clock on her laptop, "It's only five. You've got some time. Maybe a little snooze will help you shake off this mood."

That phrase "shake off this mood" reminded her of what Julie had said to her earlier, and why. Another wave of nausea rippled through Poppy's belly. She had hurt Julie, too. And Zachary. She had to lie down and think about how to face everyone.

As she closed her eyes, she realized Esme was probably in her own room doing the exact same thing.

CHAPTER FIFTEEN

An Awkward Occasion

Kay, carrying a paper bag filled with miscellaneous serving utensils and gadgets, opened the door to 2B without knocking. Sam followed, hefting a large wooden bowl filled with his famous summer salad with peaches. Grady and Esme entered, each balancing a plate full of Cauldron Cakes. Esme had begged her parents to let her stay home, but they just wouldn't budge.

Poppy, who sat on the couch shuffling UNO cards, didn't look up.

"Oooh!" Sasha took the salad from Sam. "My favorite bowl. Don't want that disappearing to California."

"Those plates are yours, too," Kay offered. "Along with everything in this bag. I can't believe how many things I'm finding."

Sasha pointed to a large box inside the front door. "Me too. That's full of your stuff. I even found a sweater of Sam's that Will must have borrowed back in the day."

"Your zebra leggings are in there too, Esme," Sasha added. "You'd better give Poppy's room a once-over for anything else, just to be safe."

Esme, still carrying the heavy plate and standing awkwardly behind Kay, just nodded.

Sasha took it from her and glanced at the oven timer. Twenty minutes until the chicken would be ready. It was going to be a very long twenty minutes if they couldn't get the girls talking.

"Wow! You weren't kidding, Kay. These Cauldron Cakes are fantastic. Check these out, Pops." Sasha was trying to pull her daughter out of her funk.

But the arrival of Esme, and dessert, had the opposite effect on Poppy.

"I guess you're feeling better now, Esme. Must have been all of that ice cream you ate yesterday," Poppy sniped under her breath.

Esme stood where she was, not even trying to defend herself; her red eyes began tearing up again. Yesterday afternoon, she was the happiest girl in the East Village. Tonight, she just wanted to disappear.

Meanwhile, the grownups were completely shocked. They'd never seen Esme speechless. And they'd never seen Poppy act so mean. They had seriously underestimated how bad things were.

"Well, this is going to be a fun night," Grady said sarcastically. "Dismay has been a real barrel of laughs since yesterday."

"Grady, enough. I thought you ladies might like to steal a few peach slices from my salad for tonight's concoction?" Sam's approach to any uncomfortable moment was to barrel right through it.

Esme pulled herself together enough to walk to the fridge and scope out the juice situation.

She found some cloudy, all-natural apple juice at the back of the fridge. Apple peach surprise? Why not? Maybe she'd make one for Poppy too as a peace offering.

Esme pulled out their favorite glittery pink cups. But before she had ice in the first glass, Poppy spoke up and replied to Sam, "No thank you, Sam. I'm having still water tonight."

"You mean regular water? Like from the tap?" Esme snapped. She was not going to miss Poppy's habit of picking up fancy words and phrases—like still water—from Sir Charles.

"Girls! Settle down! There will be no juice, no dinner, and no dessert if you can't be nice," Sasha scolded.

"Good! I'm not hungry or thirsty. And those cupcakes look gross!"

Poppy stormed into her room and slammed the door. She was hungry. She was thirsty. And dessert looked amazing. But she wasn't going to sit through a meal with Esme, who obviously didn't even feel bad. The most important thing in their lives, the whole reason for starting Peony's Prancing Pups, was those necklaces. Now they'd never be able to get them. Poppy didn't care. Tomorrow she would apologize to Julie and tell her to put the necklaces out front and center in the case for someone else to buy.

CHAPTER SIXTEEN

Pinky Promises

After a terrible night of tossing and turning, Poppy stretched and rubbed her eyes as she opened her bedroom door. Straight ahead, she could see Sasha and Kay sitting on the couch—shoulder to shoulder, heads together, whispering quietly.

Poppy rubbed her eyes again. They looked almost exactly like bigger versions of Poppy and Esme. At that moment, Poppy realized how much her mom was going to miss *her* best friend, Kay. At least Kay and Sam would have each other in California.

"Hi," Poppy said softly, not wanting to interrupt their moment.

Sasha and Kay turned around in unison.

"Morning, Peanut," Sasha said in a gentle voice. "Hungry? Kay brought blueberry muffins from Corner Café; they're in the oven staying warm."

"Okay. More coffee?"

"Sure, thanks," Kay said, holding out her mug. "Then come sit with us."

Poppy wondered if Kay was mad at her on behalf of Esme, but Kay smiled warmly as Poppy took her mug and walked into the kitchen. Poppy grabbed a muffin, poured some coffee for Kay, and sat across from them in her favorite deep gold velvet chair.

"What are you guys talking about?" Poppy asked, though she was pretty sure she knew. "Es and me?"

"Actually, no. We were talking about Kay and me," Sasha said, "and an argument we had a long time ago."

"B.C. Before Children," Kay clarified. "It was a really long time ago."

Poppy's surprise must have been obvious. She couldn't imagine them fighting at all.

"What happened?" Poppy asked, intrigued.

"Well..." Sasha started. "I made a bad choice. And I paid for it."

"I paid for it, too!" Kay added. "I spent a week being furious at you. But I missed you like crazy the whole time."

"Mama, what did you do?" Poppy asked, her eyes wide.

"I so regret this, even now. More than fifteen years later." Sasha was visibly uncomfortable. "Kay bought this gorgeous pale-yellow lace dress specially to wear for her first anniversary dinner with Sam. She left it at my apartment so she could surprise him. The day before their anniversary, I wore it to a work event without asking. And then I spilled cranberry juice all down the front. It was totally ruined. When I tried to clean it, it just got worse."

Poppy looked at her mom, shocked, and then at Kay, who was looking down into her coffee.

"Kay, what did you do?"

"I went to pick up my dress, and I flipped out. I yelled. I cried. I told your mom I hated her. And then I wouldn't talk to her." Kay sounded ashamed.

"It was an accident. But it was dumb and disrespectful of me. I knew how much you were looking forward to your anniversary. It was my fault," Sasha said apologetically.

"But I should never have said 'hate.' Of course I didn't hate you. And I was embarrassed at my behavior."

"That was the worst." Sasha shook her head. "I wanted to apologize, and you wouldn't listen. You wouldn't even pick up the phone. And that made ME mad at YOU."

"At first, I needed to cool down, and then I just dug my heels in. But then I just missed you," Kay said.

"Same! I was mad at you for saying you hated me and then giving me the silent treatment. We were so dumb. We almost ruined our friendship."

"So, how did you start talking again?" Poppy couldn't believe all this had happened over a dumb dress!

Sasha and Kay started to laugh.

"She wrote me a love note," Kay said, "and slipped it under my door."

"Since we were both acting like children, I figured that was an appropriate way to handle it," Sasha explained. "I wrote her a love note, like kids do in grammar school. It had a few important questions and a place to circle either *Yes* or *No* for each one. I started with the basics: *Do you like me?*"

"I circled *Yes*," Kay said.

"The next question was a little harder," Sasha continued, looking at Poppy, who was staring back, enthralled with the story. "*Can you forgive me?*"

Poppy turned to look at Kay, who was smiling sweetly at the memory.

"It took me a minute, but the answer was *Yes* again."

"The third question was the most important one." Sasha winked at Kay and said, "*Will you be my best friend again?*"

Sasha and Kay linked their pinkies together and recited the rest of the note in unison,

"*I pinky promise never to borrow your clothes or drink cranberry juice ever again if you pinky promise never to say you hate me or give me the silent treatment ever again. Sincerely, your best friend forever, Sasha.*"

They had clearly done this before.

"Wow," Poppy said. "Mom, is that why you always tell me to respect people's belongings? And I can't believe you got so mad over a dress, Kay. Couldn't you have worn something else?"

"A reasonable question...but it wasn't only about the dress," Sasha explained. "I had broken our trust. And then it escalated."

"Maybe a little bit like you and Esme?" Kay suggested.

"But we worked so hard for that money, and now we can't even get the necklaces. It's all her fault!" Poppy felt a little bit bad saying this to Kay.

"Esme feels sick about it, too," Sasha scolded. "She and Sam scoured the neighborhood, looking for that envelope until after nine last night."

"And I called Jimmy at Rainbow Sprinkles," Kay added. "No one found it there."

"We were having the most perfect, best summer ever. And now it's ruined," Poppy sulked.

"But why was it the most perfect, best summer ever, Pop?" Kay probed. "Was it the money and the necklaces?"

"Or was it maybe the most perfect, best summer ever because you started a business? And helped our neighbors? And had someone write an article about you?" Sasha continued.

"And spent time with your best friend," Kay added softly, "who feels really awful she made a mistake. And really misses her best friend."

"I know," Poppy sighed.

Their friendship meant more than the necklaces. She felt embarrassed thinking about how awful she'd been.

"I was really mean," Poppy confessed. "Why did I have to get so mad?"

"Sometimes when we know someone we love is leaving, we push them away to make it easier to say goodbye," Kay suggested gently. "Maybe that had something to do with it?"

Poppy thought about it. Kay was probably right. But it didn't make her feel any better.

"What do you think I should do?"

"Well, you could start by bringing Esme a muffin?" Sasha suggested, hoping if Poppy took the first step, the girls could work it out from there.

"Sam and Grady are playing basketball; she's just up there reading in her room, and the front door is open," Kay added.

Poppy looked back and forth between the two and nodded.

Esme was propped up on her bed, staring out the window, a book in her lap, when Poppy knocked.

"Hi, Es. It's me," Poppy said tentatively.

Esme turned around, surprised at the sound of Poppy's voice.

"What are you doing here?"

"I have a muffin," Poppy said, awkwardly offering it to her.

"Thanks, I like muffins," Esme replied, taking the muffin, equally awkwardly.

"It's warm," Poppy said, stating the obvious.

"Yes, it's really warm," Esme confirmed.

"It's blueberry, your favorite," Poppy added.

"Yes, that's my favorite," Esme agreed.

The Peonies glanced at each other nervously. For the

first time in their lives, they didn't know what to say to each other. Poppy stared at a few half-full moving boxes on the far side of the room. The reality of Esme packing made it even more important that she get this conversation started.

"Has your mom ever told you the yellow dress story?" Poppy asked.

Esme shook her head no while taking a big bite of muffin, careful not to get crumbs in her bed.

"Basically, a long time ago, our moms got in a dumb fight and then they made a pinky promise not to have dumb fights."

"A pinky promise? That's all it took to fix it?" Esme asked hopefully, leaning forward.

"Well...they're still friends, aren't they?" Poppy walked toward Esme's desk, but still wouldn't look her in the eyes. Usually, Esme's desk was a little bit cluttered, but today it was practically empty.

"I'm really, really sorry, Poppy. I wish I could fix it."

Poppy wasn't ready to give in quite yet. She looked at the few familiar things left on Esme's desk; a pink mug of pens and pencils, the silver heart-shaped jewelry box her Grandma Marty had given her when she turned ten, a black and white photograph of the Peonies in their fairy wings in a turquoise frame. Everything else was already packed. Poppy reached out and picked up the frame carefully.

"If I could go back in time, I would have run straight home. I wouldn't have gone to get ice cream. And I wouldn't even have *looked* at Nico!"

"That would be impossible for you," Poppy muttered, unable to resist teasing Esme about Nico, even under the circumstances.

She put down the photo and turned to peek at Esme to see her reaction. Esme was hugging her favorite stuffed polar bear tightly under one arm and clutching the muffin just as tightly in her other hand.

"Well, I wouldn't have seen him at all, because I would have been at home. Alone. With the money," Esme reasoned and continued. "Poppy, I would rather have our money back than anything in the world, but the money doesn't even matter if we're not best friends."

Poppy finally broke down. "I was so mad I said some really horrible stuff," she admitted and felt a little better as soon as she said it. It wasn't all Esme's fault, they had both been wrong. She took a few steps forward and sat down on the bed.

"You really hurt my feelings," Esme said shyly. She could act pretty tough when she wanted to and didn't like to admit when she was hurt.

"I know..." Poppy closed her eyes, remembering. "I didn't mean it."

"I got mad, too, and I'm sorry. I'm glad you came upstairs," Esme offered, and then joked, "I was really hungry."

"Me too." Poppy smiled. She couldn't stay mad, and she knew that wasn't the only reason Esme was glad she had come upstairs. It might take some time, but she thought everything would be okay.

“Walk the dogs?” Esme asked, extending her little finger.

“Let’s go,” Poppy agreed, wrapping her pinky around Esme’s.

CHAPTER SEVENTEEN

Flower Power

After a scolding from Sir Charles for being twenty minutes late and a frenetic pick-up from Liz, who shooed them out the door so she could feed the twins, The Peonies were out on the sidewalk in the oppressive August heat.

"This weather is the worst," Poppy complained. "Can you believe it actually rained yesterday?"

Esme's parents had told her that, while Southern California is hot, it's a dry heat, meaning not so sweaty. She was about to share that bit of trivia with Poppy when she stopped herself. She didn't want to make it sound like she was happy to leave.

"Good to see you out and about," Tony called to Esme.

She smiled and waved back.

Poppy thought to tease Esme that she wasn't going to get real New York pizza like Tony's in California. But she stopped herself. She didn't want to make Esme feel bad.

They walked along in silence down the block. They

were friends again, but something hung between them in the air, something other than their fight.

"Are you scared?" Poppy finally asked.

Esme knew exactly what she meant.

"Yeah, you?"

Poppy nodded. They'd always planned to face middle school, high school, and their entire lives together. Now each of them would be on her own.

"I just never thought I'd be walking into a new school all by myself one day," Esme added.

"I know. Me neither," Poppy agreed, rubbing her eyes to stop from crying. "I don't want a new best friend."

Esme knew it wasn't her fault, but she felt terrible knowing she was the reason Poppy was so sad.

"You won't need one, and you better not get one," Esme teased. "We'll talk all the time. It'll be fine, practically the same."

But she didn't believe it, and neither did Poppy. It would be different. It already was, and it was just going to keep on changing.

The familiar bells jingled as they walked into Lucky Stars. Julie looked up from her jewelry bench where she was sketching designs with a thin black marker. Scribbles came running to greet his pals.

"Glad to see you're feeling better, Esme!" Julie smiled. "And you, Poppy? How's your mood today?"

Poppy was embarrassed all over again by her behavior the day before.

"Yeah, sorry about that, Julie." She really was, and she hoped Julie could tell.

"No big thing. Just get that adorable little beast out of here. I've got an idea for a new fall line—tiny leaves on long chains, like they're falling from trees. It's going to be fabulous. I just need to concentrate and work out how to translate the concept into different pieces."

Julie got really focused when she had a new idea.

"Do me a favor," she added. "Pull some cash out of my bag and get me a small iced latte and a cinnamon roll from Drew's. Take a twenty and get yourselves each something, too."

Poppy pulled Julie's brown fringe purse out from under the counter and carefully pulled a twenty-dollar bill out of the flowered plastic pencil case she used for a wallet.

Esme wandered over to the corner of the shop where the peony necklaces were stashed. She felt overwhelmed by sadness knowing she'd blown their chances of ever owning the delicate gold pendants. There had to be a way.

"Come on, Es," Poppy called. "Let's get going before it gets any hotter."

On the short walk to Drew's Diner, Esme's stubborn streak took hold.

"There's got to be a way to make our money back!"

"I'm all ears." Poppy was willing to consider anything.

"How about...a walkathon. Like that Kids Walk for Cancer we did that time. We could walk like a hundred dogs at once."

"That was for charity, Esme. We're not a charity.

Besides, the dogs can't walk themselves. We'd have to hire other kids to help us walk a hundred dogs."

"Okay. Bad idea." She hadn't thought that one all the way through.

"Oooh!! Doggy Day Care! Ten dollars for the day!" Esme was getting excited now.

Poppy did the math. "We'd need thirty-five dogs, Esme. And where are we going to keep them? Your apartment? Even with you moving, I don't think your parents would go for that."

Esme felt defeated. Poppy was being so negative. She wasn't even trying to offer any ideas.

"You wait here. I'll go in." Poppy didn't have to ask what Esme wanted. Drew made the cinnamon rolls himself. They were giant, drenched in icing, and delicious. Even Poppy, who often preferred a piece of fruit to a slice of cake, could not resist them. They were her second favorite sweet next to ice cream.

"Sounds good, Pop. Thanks."

Poppy felt bad for shooting Esme down. But she was just being realistic. They had one week and exactly zero dollars. She placed her order with Drew, paid, and looked around the busy diner. It always made her feel good to see all of the different customers talking, enjoying their food, and admiring her dad's photos. Drew handed her the treats across the counter, interrupting her memories of that crazy fun time Will dressed them up as East Village Fairies, when suddenly, it came to her like a flash! Poppy bounded out the door, screaming.

"I'VE GOT IT!!!!!!!!!!!!"

"I'm right here, Poppy!"

"Sorry! I'm just so excited!"

Poppy stood, holding a big pink box and balancing a tray with three drinks—one coffee and two lemonades—with an enormous smile on her face.

"Okay…?" Esme was curious, Poppy had gone from totally negative to THIS in a matter of minutes. And Poppy was not usually the dramatic one of the pair.

"A puppy photo booth!" Poppy announced proudly and waited for Esme to embrace her idea.

Esme considered it for a moment, but she needed more details.

"Go on…" she encouraged.

"We set up near the dog run."

Esme nodded. This one had potential. "Make a cool background; bring props," she suggested.

"Exactly!" Poppy bounced on the balls of her feet with excitement. "We can even bring our old…"

"…fairy wings!" Esme finished, knowing exactly what Poppy was about to say. "We can borrow your mom's old phone to take the pictures. The cracked one she uses to play music…"

"We could charge five bucks for a mini-photo shoot," Poppy added. "People can pick what they like, and we can email them later."

“It would be better if we could print them...” Esme was hooked.

Poppy nodded, handing the tray of drinks to Esme. “Good point.”

Esme’s eyes lit up as she took the tray. “We can even sell lemonade. No...”

The girls looked at each other and excitedly, in unison, shouted, “Passionfruit iced tea!!”

“Okay. Good one!” Poppy’s organizational side continued to simmer “Let’s bring Julie her breakfast, then head to the park and make a plan.”

By the time they got back to their building, the girls had a rough plan outlined. They decided on Friday, the day before Esme left. That would give them time to get ready, and they couldn’t think of a better way to spend their last day together in New York. They’d do it midday when it was hottest, so they could sell the most tea. They’d have free treats for the doggies to help attract passersby. They’d raid their dress-up box and old clothes for funny props and costumes. And they’d call it *Peony’s Pop-Up Picture Parlor for Pups.*

They burst into Esme’s apartment to retrieve their old dress-up box and found Sam and Will, sitting on the couch—shoulder to shoulder, heads together, whispering quietly—just like Poppy had found Kay and Sasha that morning. Poppy sometimes forgot the only reason they all knew one another was because her dad and Sam had met in college.

"Where's the fire?" Sam made the worst jokes.

"Dads!" Esme sometimes called them Dads because she knew they loved it. Will hadn't been around much this summer, so she'd rarely had the chance. "We have the BEST idea ever!"

"Can't wait to hear it!" said Will.

Poppy and Esme laid the whole thing out carefully, being certain to show how well they'd thought it through. When they finally finished, they waited for a reaction.

"Genius!" Sam exclaimed.

"Brilliant," Will agreed, "but you don't have to use Sasha's old iPhone. I've got a terrific point-and-shoot digital camera you can borrow. Very professional."

"Have you thought about how you'll get the word out?" Sam was the joker of the group, but also a good planner.

"A sign at Lucky Stars and some flyers in the park?" Poppy was worried it wasn't enough but was so happy Esme was on board with her idea, she hadn't wanted to be negative.

"Great idea," Sam encouraged, then added, "and how about I call Milo and give him an exclusive scoop? A follow-up article on the neighborhood blog should help boost attendance."

What a great idea! Why hadn't they thought of that?

The four put their heads together and banged out final details. It was fun to be scheming with their dads again—even if it might be the last time for a while.

"I know a photo supplier who's trying to unload some overstock frames at a really great price. You could decorate them and include the frame with a printout," Will suggested.

"I bet we could charge ten dollars!" Esme loved the idea.

Poppy loved the idea, too, but it had a flaw. "Good idea, Dad. But how will we pay for the frames?"

Will paused, "You know what? Let me worry about that. The frames won't add up to much, and they'll be my donation to the cause. I can lend you a printer, too, and throw in the photo paper. I've got plenty lying around at the studio."

Sam turned to Will and asked, "Is the camera wi-fi enabled?"

Will nodded. "Yep. I've never tried to use it, but it said so on the box."

"Do you think Julie would be willing to let people pick up their framed prints from her shop on their way home?" Sam asked, rubbing his chin—a definite sign his thinking cap was on. "We could send the images digitally and keep the frames and printer there, a safe distance from all the wagging tails."

"Ooooh," Poppy jumped in, "maybe some of the people will shop while they're there. She'll say yes for sure if it means bringing in more people."

Sam made a note. "I'll add Julie to my list of calls. What else?"

"We have all of the props and art supplies we need, and plenty of doggie treats. We'll just have to get tea and cups." Poppy started adding the costs up in her head.

Sam got up, ran into the kitchen, and retrieved a sun tea dispenser filled with Corner Café passionfruit tea bags. "All packed up and ready for the move. We've got plenty of paper cups, too. Consider it *my* donation to the cause."

"Thanks, Dads. This is great!" Things were really coming together with their help and donations.

"Just one more thing…" Sam sounded serious. What had they forgotten?

"Can we come help?" he asked. "We won't get in the way. You can treat us just like employees."

Esme liked the idea of bossing their dads around. "Actually, why don't you guys man the pick-up station? Print the photos and put them in the frames?"

Esme was genius. They loved their dads, but they didn't want them looking over their shoulders all day!

"It's a deal," Sam agreed.

"I'm in, too." Will got a funny, faraway look on his face. "This will be my last chance to see my favorite two ladies in action for a very long while."

Every time The Peonies started to forget, someone brought up Esme's move. Thank goodness Sam was there to barrel right through it.

“Come on, you guys.” Sam put his arm out. “Give me a cheer.”

They each placed a hand on top of his, and all together, they did the father-daughter cheer they’d been doing before recitals, sporting events, and school tests for years.

“Gimme a P. Gimme an E. Gimme an awesome Peony! Goooooo Peonies!!! Now kick some butt!!”

The girls giggled and ran to Esme’s room to continue their planning.

CHAPTER EIGHTEEN

Old Dogs, New tricks

Poppy and Esme leaned over the counter at Lucky Stars, furiously working on customizing fifty frames for the photo booth.

The girls had created a map of Tompkins Square Park with a hole in the middle, shaped just like the dog run, so a photo could shine through. They had traced the maps on heavy foam core, cut them out, and painted them with trees and flowers.

"I'm so glad your dad was able to get us these frames from his photo supply friend!" Esme said, not looking up from her work.

"I bet the guy was happy to get rid of them. Who would buy this?" Poppy said, holding up a tacky fake gold plastic frame. "But they're perfect for us."

When they had finished painting the park cut-outs, they glued them to the frames, covering the cheap plastic—no one would know how ugly they were underneath.

"Ta-Da!" Esme held up a completed custom frame. "A one-of-a-kind, handmade Tompkins Square Park Dog Run frame for your fur baby's photo!"

As they dried, Poppy carefully wrote "Dog Days of Summer at Tompkins Square Park" on each one in her meticulous handwriting with a silver paint pen.

"Looking good, Poppy!" Esme encouraged. "Just fourteen more to go."

"Better finish those up, girls!" Julie said, looking up from her computer. "Milo just messaged he'll be posting the story in a few minutes. I think you're going to be very busy!"

"Don't pressure me!" Poppy begged. "I'll mess up. Talk about something else."

"Hmmmm...back-to-school shopping?" Julie suggested, always interested in fashion and curious to hear what trends the girls were into.

"Well, speaking of Milo, we *have* been thinking about backpacks," Poppy said, still focusing intently on her work. "Milo has a really cool one...it has tons of pockets, includes a matching water bottle, and he said it comes in all different crazy colors and patterns."

"And I really want Doc Martens," Esme said. Liz had several pairs of Doc Marten boots and said they weren't just super cool, but also super comfortable.

"Oooh, me too!" Poppy agreed, hoping they made them in her petite size.

"We need sneakers, too. Chuck Taylors again?" Esme asked.

"Obviously! Converse are the best," Poppy replied quickly "OH! What about our winter coats? What color should we get this year? I feel like hot pink, or maybe mix it up and go with blue?"

"Hmmm...I think stick with pink," Esme replied. "It's our signature shade, after all," she added, flipping her long shiny locks behind her shoulders dramatically.

Poppy laughed. But Julie looked at them sadly. Then it dawned on Esme. She wasn't going to need a winter coat in Southern California.

By the change in Poppy's expression, from beaming smile to sullen frown, Esme could tell her BFF was thinking the same thing. But before the mood shifted completely, Julie exclaimed, "Girls, the article is live!"

The Peonies bolted upright, practically threw their art supplies aside, and ran to join Julie behind the counter.

"What does it say?" Poppy said.

"Is there a photo?" asked Esme.

They squeezed in tight on either side of Julie, leaning in to read the blog post.

Dog Days of Summer Heading for a Photo Finish!

Esme and Poppy, the entrepreneurial girls behind Peony's Prancing Pups, are at it again! As reported here earlier this summer, The Peonies have been operating their dog walking business successfully since late June. But for one day only, the girls will be offering a special doggie treat!

This Friday, from 11 a.m. – 3 p.m., right by the Tompkins Square Park dog run, stop by Peony's Pop-Up Picture Parlor for Pups—a photo booth for dogs! Come by during your lunch break or bring a picnic and stick around to see who is Best in Show.

"We made such good friends here this summer running PPP, meeting all the neighborhood dogs and their owners, we figured it would be a great way to capture those memories forever," explained Esme, who is moving to California in just a couple of days, "and have a good time doing it."

"We are making it extra fun by offering a selection of costumes and props for people to choose from," Poppy added. "And each photo comes in a custom-designed, hand-painted frame."

Assisted by well-known local photographer Will (who also happens to be Poppy's dad), the photos will be sent digitally to Lucky Stars gift shop, printed, and available for pick up within five minutes. Each framed quality print is just $10!

This seems like another successful business venture for The Peonies. Who says you can't teach old dogs new tricks?

"Yayyy!" Esme whooped. "Milo totally came through! And the photo is awesome. Liz nailed our hair!"

Liz had done their hair for the shoot, two ponytails with streaks of hot pink running through them. They stood with their arms around each other, beaming in their PPP t-shirts holding Chunky between them. Behind them was the special backdrop they had created for the photo booth: pale blue with wisps of white dabbed on with a big sponge—it looked like a perfect summer sky.

“I think you guys have been spending too much time with the dogs—you’re starting to look like them! Poppy’s curly puffs look like poodle ears, and your sleek ponytails look like spaniel ears, Esme!” Julie remarked.

“That’s the point!” Esme laughed. “In honor of two of our favorite clients, Scribbles and Precious!”

“Well, you’re right, then...Liz did nail it,” Julie agreed. “Really cute.”

“Let’s get back to work, Es,” Poppy said, heading back to the worktable and grabbing her paintbrush. “I have a feeling Julie’s right. We’re going to be very busy!”

CHAPTER NINETEEN

A Photo Finish

The Peonies had taken over a sunny corner of the park for the photo booth. They commandeered three benches in a row across from the dog run, right on the main walkway, and tied pink balloons to the arms of the benches.

"Wow, everyone, this looks terrific!" Kay said, giving Sam a playful kiss on the cheek.

Sam barely looked up. He was engrossed in connecting Will's camera to the printer at Lucky Stars.

The cheerful backdrop hung tightly between two poles, behind the middle park bench, creating a stage. The girls had used bright sidewalk chalk to create "walls" around their area and make it even more festive.

"Thanks, Mom," Esme said. "It's cool, right? The costume display was Poppy's idea." Esme was on her hands and knees adding some final touches to the sidewalk art.

A rope was stretched between two trees and peppered with colorful costumes: scarves, boas, hats, gloves, sunglasses, tutus, and mermaid tails, all attached with wooden clothespins.

Poppy pulled a blue and white gingham dress out of her bag. "Look, my old Dorothy costume!" she exclaimed, clipping it to the rope. "I still love *The Wizard of Oz*."

"I'll get you, my pretty! And your little dog, too!" Sasha joked, grabbing a witch hat from the line and wrapping her arms around Poppy.

Kay whipped on a pair of the fairy wings, flapped her arms, and swooped toward Esme, squealing like one of the evil flying monkeys.

"Moms, would you stop messing around and stand in front of the backdrop for a minute?" Will asked from behind the camera, which was now set up on a tripod about ten feet away from the stage. "I just want to check the light."

Kay and Sasha immediately struck a pose. They were all used to being Will's models.

"Okay! We're in business," Will said. "The light looks great, and the shot is all set up. You just have to hit the button like I showed you."

The girls nodded.

Sam took over from Will behind the camera and explained, "Then you just select the photo you want, press print, and the camera sends it right over."

"But how will we know..." Poppy started to ask when Sam's phone buzzed, announcing the arrival of a text.

"Confirmation from Julie," Sam smiled. "We're good to go. Now Will and I can retire to Lucky Stars, crank the AC, put our feet up, and relax!"

"DAD!!" Esme objected. "You can't relax! You have to put the photos in frames! You're working for us today."

"I don't know...I think we've done enough. There's a game on, isn't there, Will?" Sam teased.

"No way, Dads," Poppy said. "You are both on the clock today. Kay helped with the backdrop, and Mom helped with the costumes!"

"Totally kidding, kiddos," Sam said. "Happy to work backstage today with my main man! Proud to be an honorary Peony!"

"We're on park patrol. Just call if you have any hiccups with the printer," Sasha said, hanging the witch hat back on the line and pointing to a grassy spot close by. "We'll be right over there."

"Hey, are you guys open or what?" said a familiar voice.

The girls spun around to see Grady and Nico standing there with Chunky.

"What the...?" Esme wondered aloud.

"Don't worry, sis, I'm not trying to get in on your dog-walking turf. We ran into Liz in the lobby on her way over here. She forgot something upstairs, so we said we'd take Chunk," Grady explained.

"It was either Chunky or the twins!" Nico joked. "Hey, this looks great, you guys. Nice hair, too." Liz had recreated their puppy ear ponytails for the occasion—with extra pink streaks.

"Thanks, Nico. Hey, we're almost ready, do you guys

want to be our first shot?" Poppy asked.

"Yeah! C'mon, Grady. Let's do it. Just me and Grady though. No offense, Chunky," Nico said, handing Chunky's leash to Poppy.

"We'll send two prints so you guys can each have one," Esme offered.

"That would be awesome. Thanks, Es," Grady said. "This does look really good. The balloons are a nice touch."

"Okay! Places! Just sit on the bench, or stand up. Whatever feels natural," Esme directed as Poppy stood by, both looking at the camera's display. As always, Nico was smiling from ear to ear. Grady sucked in his cheeks, pouted, and stared into the camera seriously, like he was a runway model.

"Grady, please smile. What's with the face?" Kay scolded.

"Geez, G-Dog the model!" Will teased. "Way to work that camera."

Grady burst into laughter just as Esme snapped the photo, a great shot of great friends. Poppy pressed send, and it was on the way to the printer at Lucky Stars.

"Okay. It's 11:01! Parents out. Boys out," Sam declared, checking his watch.

"We'll be in our spot if you need us," Kay said, gesturing at the lawn behind them. "Good luck!"

And with that, *Peony's Pop-Up Picture Parlor for Pups* was in business.

"Hey, girls. Looks like you're ready to get this party started!" Liz waved as she approached, pushing her double stroller. Chunky started wiggling his tail as soon as he heard her voice. "Hey, Mr. Chunk. Are you ready for your close-up?"

Chunky wagged his tail even harder as Liz examined all of the costume choices.

"Hey, Liz!" Esme called. "Actually, we have something special picked out for you."

Poppy reached into her bag and pulled out a pair of red glitter sunglasses shaped like a lightning bolt and a bandanna with the British flag printed on it.

"In honor of Mr. Bowie!" Poppy explained.

"Wow, you girls have really been paying attention all these years. Or am I actually that obsessed with David Bowie?" Liz questioned with a smile.

"Both!" Esme laughed. "You are totally obsessed! Let's do it!"

Poppy placed Chunky on the bench, wrapped the scarf around his neck so most of the design showed on his back, and propped the sunglasses on his nose. Hilarious!

"Good boy, Chunky. Sit. Stay." Poppy held her right hand up, palm toward him, and showed him a treat in her left hand. "That's a good boy. Okay. Now, Esme!"

"Perfect! Got it!" Esme cheered. "What a good boy."

Poppy handed Chunk the treat and removed his

costume before he even realized he was wearing it. Liz handed Poppy a ten-dollar bill, which she tucked quickly into her pink fanny pack.

"Thanks, Liz. Nice doing business with you!"

"My pleasure! We'll see you a little later." Liz waved goodbye.

Julie and Scribbles approached just then. "Hey, all! Wanted to get my photo in the queue before it gets mobbed. And I've got a couple of old guys watching the store."

"Awesome! Take a look at our options while I help these thirsty folks!" Esme said. "Hello everyone! Can I interest anyone in some iced tea?"

A small crowd had started to form, drawn in by the balloons, the backdrop, and the East Village Update article. Some had dogs who wagged their tails and sniffed each other as the humans eyed the costume selection. The non-dog owners offered opinions about both the dogs and the costumes. It was a pretty festive scene!

"Okay. This is perfect!" Julie declared, holding up a black studded leather bracelet from Poppy's punk rock Halloween costume a couple of years back. "It'll fit around Scribble's neck easily!"

"Oooh, that's funny," Esme yelled from the iced tea station. "That'll be one dollar each, folks."

"This outfit will capture his tough-guy personality," Poppy said, stepping behind the camera. "Ready, Scribbles? Say 'Kibbles'!"

"Kibbles!" Julie and The Peonies said together.

At that moment, Scribbles stood up on his hind legs, like he was trying to intimidate someone.

"Got it! Good one, Scribbles!" Poppy said as Scribbles ran toward her to collect his treat.

"Here's your dough," Julie said, forking over two fives. "I'm going to take advantage of my shop boys and take a little walk with my tough guy Scribbles before things get busy!"

"Thanks for everything, Julie," Poppy said sincerely. "Hopefully, if business keeps up like this, we'll be by Lucky Stars later to make our big purchase!!"

"I've got a good feeling about it," Julie confirmed.

"Okay, folks, everyone has a drink...now who's next on the runway?" Esme asked, addressing the handful of people crowding around their setup.

The Peonies had a solid stream of friendly people (and dogs) coming through. They knew some of the visitors from the dog run or the neighborhood, but there were lots of new faces, too. Something about a dog in a costume made everyone smile. How could it not? With each photo they took, and every ten dollars they stashed in their fanny packs, they drew a line with chalk on the sidewalk to keep a running tally. They were up to nineteen when a familiar voice said, “Well, it looks like the article did its job!”

Milo walked toward them, his dreads in a big bunch on top of his head. He was holding hands with a tall woman with matching dreadlocks, also piled on top of her head. And she was holding a leash, walking Thor, Scribbles' favorite playmate from the dog run. Thor started wagging his tail as he got closer to The Peonies.

“I see you know my boy!” Milo said. “Do you know Thor's mom, Amy?”

“Wait, you're Thor's dad?” Esme blurted out. “We've been watching him play with Scribbles all summer and could never figure out who his owner was!”

Amy smiled shyly. “I'm Amy. Nice to meet you.”

“But where were you?” Poppy asked, puzzled. “Who was with Thor?”

“My spot is all the way in the back corner,” Amy explained, “behind the trees and the doggie pool, where old tennis balls go to die.”

“Amy is a writer, too—short stories,” Milo explained. “She brainstorms at the dog run, says she totally gets in her zone there, but not if she's making small talk. She's the one who told me about you two.”

“I don't really like to chit chat, but I do like to observe,” Amy said. “I love the people watching in the park—it's where I get some of my best characters!”

"Us, too!" The Peonies said in unison. "We love people watching!"

"Speaking of characters, you guys better get back to your customers." Milo gestured at the still gathering crowd.

"Thor first," Poppy insisted, grabbing a grass skirt from the display. "I have an idea."

She quickly twisted and braided and sectioned off the grass skirt, then plopped it on Thor's head.

"Quick, Esme. Before Thor's dreads fall off!" Poppy exclaimed.

"Awesome! Got it," Esme said. "Hilarious. Like father, like son!"

"Well, thanks, girls. I'll miss watching you," Amy said, reaching into her purse to pay for their photo.

"Let us know if we ever make it into one of your short stories," Poppy said, excited at the prospect.

The Peonies looked at each other with wonder—how had they missed her all summer? And how cool would it be to be in a short story? They had a lot to debrief! But first, back to work.

A casual line had formed. Todd stood patiently at the front, chatting with everyone as always, while Tab used up every inch of slack on his leash to herd the other waiting dogs.

"Always working, huh, Tab?" Poppy laughed. "And you, too, Todd, working the line, chatting everyone up. I love today's shirt. You look extra handsome!" And he did. Todd wore a bright orange shirt with white flowers, yellow pineapples, and brown tiki masks. He'd paired it with crisp white linen pants and brown sandals.

"Thanks, Poppy. This is a special one," Todd said. "I think the orange makes my eyes pop. Don't you agree?"

"Indeed!" Poppy nodded enthusiastically. "And I've got just the thing for Tab!" She held up a couple of items from the costume rack—a tiny cowboy hat and a red bandanna. "Best ranch hand in the East Village," she proclaimed while getting Tab all gussied up.

"Yee haa!!" Esme exclaimed from behind the camera. "That was a great shot!"

"Thanks, Peonies!" Todd said. "I think Tab and I will take in some sun and see who else shows up today. Looks like you're on track!"

Todd and Tab grabbed a bench nearby as The Peonies made their way through the line, which was at least ten people long, taking shot after shot after shot. Some with costumes, some without. Some with their owners, but mostly without. These photos were all about the dogs. The whole time, they doled out passionfruit iced tea—the big dispenser was almost empty, and they had only nine cups left. (The secret was out—passionfruit was the best flavor of all!) Everyone was having a great time.

When the line dwindled down, the girls took advantage of the break in the action to tidy up the costumes and props. It looked like a tornado had blown through them.

"Esme, it kind of looks like your bedroom!" Poppy teased as she rehung items on the clothesline.

"I see you have some excellent habits, Peonies. Cleaning as you go leaves less work at the end. A tidy workspace is a profitable workspace."

The Peonies automatically straightened their shoulders at the sound of Sir Charles' voice.

"Absolutely!" said Poppy.

"It's like you taught us," Esme added. "If there's time to lean, there's time to clean!"

They turned around and there stood Sir Charles in a crisp blue and white striped seersucker summer suit and a red bow tie. A straw boater hat with a red and navy grosgrain ribbon topped off his outfit, and in his arms, as always, was Precious.

And, Precious was, for the first time ever, not wearing something that matched Sir Charles' outfit! To the girls' surprise, Princess Precious was wearing a doggie shirt, covered with bright red tropical flowers, big green palm leaves, and pink flamingos, all on an aqua background. Instead of her typical understated bows, there was a big red flower clipped to one ear. The Peonies looked at each other in disbelief—what was going on? Precious looked adorable, but she was barely recognizable. Should they say something?

"When you've got a moment, I'd like to engage your services for a photo of Precious," Sir Charles requested formally.

"Now is perfect," Esme said. "Take a look at our accouterments, see if anything strikes your fancy."

Poppy stared at Esme—accouterments? Strikes your fancy? Now who was the one using fancy language like Sir Charles? She couldn't wait to tease Esme.

"I'm impressed, Esme," Sir Charles said, nodding in approval. "Your vocabulary is formidable, and your collection of accouterments—from the French word for 'personal clothing and equipment,' by the way—is delightful. But as you may have noticed, I've brought my own, if that's permissible. I have a special vision in mind for our portrait—it's for...a friend."

"Sure thing. The customer is always right," Poppy said, turning her attention to take a really good look at Precious.

"One more thing!" Esme said. "I think this will complete the look!"

She pulled a pink lei from the clothesline and offered it to Sir Charles, who draped it around Precious' neck.

"Perfect," he said. "She's ready." He placed Precious on the bench. She looked like a 1950s surfer girl. With fur.

"Three, two, one...done!" Poppy said as she snapped the photo. "You can pick it up at Lucky Stars in about five minutes."

"Thank you, Peonies," Sir Charles said, handing Poppy

a neatly folded ten-dollar bill, "but I think we'll say hello to Todd and Tab first." He glanced toward the nearby bench, where Todd was sitting, watching Tab playfully lunging at birds and squirrels.

Sir Charles scooped up Precious and joined Todd. They shared a friendly hug, and Todd took Precious from Sir Charles' arms and gave her a big kiss. As they leaned in close to each other, Todd whispered something to Sir Charles, and they both threw their heads back laughing loudly. They'd never seen Sir Charles so happy and unreserved. What was going on?

"I knew they were friends," Poppy said tentatively, "but they seem like more than friends, don't you think?"

"Definitely," Esme said. "There's only one reason Sir Charles would put Precious in a Hawaiian shirt. TRUE LOVE."

"Well, Todd is awesome. And Sir Charles is a lot cooler than people think. And they're both single," Poppy reasoned.

"And they both love dogs," Esme added. "They just seem so different!"

Poppy looked at her best friend. She looked at her blond hair and pale skin and thought about her outgoing, have-no-fear attitude.

"You know what they say," Poppy said, smiling at Esme. "Opposites attract. I think it's perfect."

Esme looked at her watch and checked their tally on the sidewalk. It was 2:47 p.m., and there were thirty chalk marks, which meant thirty photos. They were so close! The girls sat down on the bench for the first time in hours.

"Hello, Peonies. Are you still open? You advertised until three. Madeline and I don't want to miss out." Suzanne was all business, all the time, which the girls had learned really was a huge benefit for the dog run. The neighborhood was lucky to have her.

Esme stood right up and confirmed, "Of course, Suzanne. As advertised. Hiya, Madeline." Esme squatted down to snuggle with Madeline—they had grown pretty tight over the summer.

"Would you like to pick a costume or a prop?" Poppy asked. "We have some really cute stuff."

"Do you have any recommendations?" Suzanne asked. "You're the professionals."

"Do you want to be in the photo too?" Esme asked hopefully, for she actually did have an idea.

"Umm, sure…I guess…" Suzanne sounded unconvinced.

Esme grabbed the two pairs of fairy wings, handed one to Suzanne, and started to put the other pair on Madeline. Poppy grinned, knowing exactly what Esme was thinking.

"Here, let me help you," Poppy offered, reaching behind

Suzanne to adjust the shoulder straps. "Do you recognize these wings?"

"Wait...are these the wings from the 'Fairy Village' photos your dad did?" Suzanne asked incredulously.

"The very same," Poppy said. "We've had them for years."

"How amazing. These really represented an important part of our neighborhood," Suzanne said, adjusting her wings.

"Well, then you should be photographed wearing them," Poppy said. "You work so hard for the dog run."

"You're like the fairy godmother for East Village dogs!" Esme chimed in. "We really got to see that this summer."

"Gee, thanks, girls. That means a lot," Suzanne said softly. She might even have had a tear in her eye. "Okay, ready when you are."

Esme and Poppy both stood behind the camera, and Suzanne couldn't help but flash a huge smile. She sat on the bench, Madeline jumped in her lap, and their glittery wings tangled together just as Esme snapped the photo. It was a magical moment.

"That's a wrap," Suzanne said, peeling off the wings. "You girls did a good thing today. This is a special place. It's nice for people to have a special memento."

"Thanks, Suzanne. It was a win-win," Esme said, taking the wings. "It was a really special way for us to spend the last day of our last summer together."

"For now, right?" Poppy objected. "It won't be our last

summer together ever..."

The Peonies got quiet for a moment as Suzanne and Madeline walked away. But they rallied quickly. There was no time to be sad right now. Poppy folded up the costumes and gathered the balloons while Esme took down the backdrop and packed up the camera.

"Hey, Pop. It's time. Let's check the tally."

"Okay," Poppy said, shoving a purple feather boa into her bag. "Do you think we did it?"

Together they leaned over the chalk tick marks on the sidewalk and counted.

"Twenty-seven, twenty-eight, twenty-nine, thirty, thirty-one!" they said together.

"At ten dollars each, that should be $310, not including the iced tea money..." Esme glanced over to make sure their moms were nearby, then started pulling dollar bills out of her fanny pack.

Poppy unzipped her own fanny pack and started counting.

The girls looked at each other with anticipation.

"Okay. I have $187," Esme said nervously.

"And I have... $194," Poppy said, obviously adding in her head. "That's a grand total of $381!!!"

"We did it!" Esme exploded, "WEEE DIIIID IIIIT!!!!!!"

People in the park whipped their heads around to see what the racket was about, but for once, Poppy didn't care. She just threw her arms around Esme. This was the perfect time for Esme's outside voice.

CHAPTER TWENTY

P & E, BFF

The Peonies awkwardly, but happily, did their favorite old choreographed Hokey Pokey dance as they headed toward Lucky Stars—pulling a heavy, overflowing wagon, bobbing a bunch of balloons, *and* dancing wasn't as easy as it sounded.

"Careful, Poppy!" Esme shouted. "Tutu overboard!"

"Not on my watch," Poppy said, scooping up the pink tulle ball before it even hit the ground.

They bumped over bricks and swerved around twigs, carefully balancing their supplies, laughing, and singing all the way to Lucky Stars.

Zachary sat outside Corner Café, his smile widening as they got closer.

"So, I'm guessing it was a success?"

"Totally!" Esme said, "And the iced tea sales put us over the top."

"Yeah, I think you'll definitely have a few new

customers!" Poppy added.

"That's good to hear, and congratulations, girls," Zachary said. "Don't you have some business to take care of with Julie?"

The girls grinned at each other—everyone knew about the necklaces. It felt good.

"You know it!" Esme said. "Some very serious Peony business."

The girls clasped hands and entered the shop—the bells tinkled, Scribbles barked, and Julie looked up at them from her workbench—just like always, but this time it felt like it was different. They knew it would be the last time for a while, at least, and they didn't want this moment to end.

"Well, well, well...judging from those smiles and the much smaller stack of frames sitting over there," Julie said as she walked to the counter, "I'm guessing you hit your goal."

"We did it, Julie!" Poppy exclaimed. "We MORE than did it!"

"We made $381! Can you believe it?" Esme said, grabbing Scribbles and hugging him tightly. "What do you think of that, boy? And it was all because of that first walk we took you on!"

Scribbles yipped and licked Esme's face.

"So, can I interest you ladies in anything today?" Julie teased. "I have some lovely candles, maybe some notecards? Oh, a magnet perhaps?"

"Julie! Knock it off!" Poppy objected, pulling a wad of

bills out of her fanny pack and slapping it on the counter. "You know exactly what we want."

"Scribs, attack!" Esme ordered jokingly, putting down Scribbles so she could add her money to the pile. "The Peonies will not be mocked!"

Julie laughed and gathered the money into one neat stack. "Call off the dog, Peonies. Let me ring you up."

The Peonies leaned on the counter anxiously as Julie organized the bills by denomination, counting as she went.

"Great, so like you said, you have $381 here..." Julie confirmed, punching buttons on her calculator. "Two rose gold peony necklaces, found buried at the bottom of a teacup."

The Peonies glanced at each other. How long had she known what they were up to?

"At $175 each," Julie continued. "That's $350, minus twenty percent—ten percent good neighbor discount, and ten percent employee discount as the Lucky Stars official dog walker. Add $24.85 in tax...The grand total comes to $304.85."

The girls ran around to the back of the counter and practically jumped on Julie with joy. Julie braced herself and threw her arms around both girls.

"Thank you, Julie! We weren't expecting an employee discount!" Esme said. "You're the best!"

"And sorry we hid the necklaces..." Poppy said. "It was just...they felt like ours, even when they weren't."

"Well," Julie said, "now they are." She reached under the counter and pulled out two Lucky Stars jewelry boxes, each wrapped in the signature style, with a little extra hot pink ribbon.

They opened their boxes in perfect sync and pulled out the necklaces. Somehow the rose gold felt different in their hands as they turned the pendants over and over between their fingers. They noticed something at the same time, but Esme, as usual, was the first to speak.

"P&E," she read softly, "BFF."

"You engraved them for us..." Poppy whispered. "But what if we weren't able to buy them?"

"I knew you could do it," Julie stated, hugging the girls. "As soon as I saw the determination in your eyes the first time you walked Scribbles, I knew these necklaces would be yours. I'm really proud of you both."

The Peonies fastened each other's necklaces on as Julie counted a few bills off the top of the pile.

"Guess you guys can split this extra seventy-six dollars? Back-to-school supplies, maybe?" Julie suggested.

Esme and Poppy looked at each other knowingly and shook their heads. Without even needing to discuss it, they knew what they wanted to do with the money.

"We want to donate it—" said Esme.

"—to the dog run," Poppy finished.

"It makes so many people, and dogs, happy!" Esme added. "We had an awesome summer there!"

"Is Suzanne the one who keeps track of the money?"

Poppy asked. "Can you give it to her?"

"Wow, girls." Julie was genuinely moved. "I'm even more proud of you. That is a really cool thing to do."

"Maybe they can buy new garbage cans, with lids that actually stay on and keep the smell contained!" Esme said.

"Let's hope so, Es," Julie laughed. "Now, get out of here! I've got some work to wrap up before I crash your family dinner!"

Scribbles jumped up into Julie's lap and the three almost-sisters and little dog smooshed together in a group hug—a Scribbles sandwich—one last time.

CHAPTER TWENTY-ONE

It takes a Village

Poppy and Esme still couldn't believe how well the day had turned out. A total success. Talk about turning lemons into lemonade—or in their case, into necklaces and passionfruit iced tea!

They rushed home, dragging their wagon, waving to neighbors along the way. Esme started thinking about how it was the last time they'd ever get to do this. But it wasn't. She'd be back to visit. They'd hang out at Lucky Stars, get ice cream, go to the park...

"Hey, Pops, slow down." Esme was suddenly overwhelmed by a tangle of different emotions. Proud and excited about the success of *Peony's Pop-Up Picture Parlor for Pups.* Lucky to have the bestest best friend in the whole wide world. Happy to have their matching necklaces. But also, really, really sad about leaving. And scared not knowing what her new life would be like.

As always, Poppy could read her mind. "It's okay, Es. Don't be sad. We had such a great day. You'll be back to visit. And I'll visit you. And it'll be great in California. I'm sure it will."

The two walked arm in arm the rest of the way, savoring their last walk to the building while it was still Esme's home, too.

The whole gang was waiting for them in 2B—Sasha, Kay, Sam, Will, Grady, and even Nico.

"Hey, you two," Will greeted them enthusiastically. "We were just talking about how terrific today was. You guys really pulled it off."

"With help from our friend-family," Poppy pointed out.

"Yeah, thanks, everyone. Thanks so much!" Esme added.

Kay started to tear up with a combination of pride and sadness. They were such great kids.

"What do you have there?" Sam pointed to the empty Lucky Stars bag to create a distraction. He couldn't take any more tears, and he had a pretty good idea how the girls' day had ended.

"We got our necklaces!" Esme answered proudly. "Julie even engraved them with our initials and BFF."

The girls were walking around the room, showing everyone their necklaces, when Esme noticed her suitcase in the corner. She felt a sudden panic.

"But we're not leaving until tomorrow! You

promised!"

"Relax," Kay soothed. "The moving truck came this morning while you guys were setting up. There's nothing left upstairs except a couple of sleeping bags and an air mattress. We thought you might like to stay here. Your brother is going over to Nico's."

"You guys are welcome to stay," Sasha offered. "I can take the couch."

"Naw." Sam put his arm around Kay. "We spent our first night in that apartment in sleeping bags fifteen years ago. It'll be kind of romantic."

"Except your back was fifteen years younger then," Will pointed out. "Good luck in the morning!"

"That's why we have the air mattress!"

They all laughed. Sam and Kay had an ongoing argument about exercise. She wanted him to try yoga to help his back. He preferred just to pop an aspirin and complain. A night on the floor would guarantee a whole lot of complaining on the first day of their cross-country drive tomorrow. Hopefully, the air mattress would help.

"Before we eat, we have something for you," said Sasha. "We're so proud of what you've done this summer, and we know the separation is going to be tough. We thought this would help."

Kay handed them each a box wrapped in purple polka dot paper with a dark purple bow.

The size and shape of the boxes were very promising.

The girls looked at each other. Could it be?

"You first, Es," Poppy was too nervous to open hers.

Esme was too excited not to. She untied and tossed the ribbon, then tore at the carefully folded and taped wrapping.

"PHONES!!!"

Even Grady smiled, remembering how happy he'd been when he first got his.

"But..." Poppy couldn't believe it.

"I know we said you had to wait until you're twelve. But we all talked about it"—Sasha gestured to all of the adults, including Will—"and we think you've earned them a little early."

A little early? Their birthdays weren't until next spring!

"Grady, can you—" Esme started to ask her brother to help them get their phones set up, when the front door buzzer rang.

"Already done. I even put photos in with everyone's numbers. I'll show you anything you need to know after we eat."

Poppy and Esme suddenly noticed that there wasn't any food cooking.

"PIZZA?!?!"

Poppy rushed to buzz their delivery into the building, threw the apartment door open, and waited.

Tony himself came off the elevator carrying three large pizza boxes.

"Tony! We didn't know you were shorthanded," Kay apologized. "We could have sent the girls."

"I'm not. I just wanted to deliver this family dinner myself. It's on the house."

Sasha and Nico got out plates and napkins. Poppy pulled the apple juice and soda water out of the fridge.

Tony hugged Kay and Esme and shook hands with Sam and Grady. "Good luck."

When Julie and Scribbles passed him in the hallway on his way out, Julie thought she saw Tony fighting back a tear.

"All right, gang. Enough moping. I'm starved!" Julie announced as she walked in the door. She was determined to keep the mood upbeat. "Did you girls show everyone your awesome score?"

Poppy and Esme nodded, both caught devouring their first bite of pizza.

"Ha! Looks like you're hungry, too!" she said. She then turned to Kay and whispered, "Did you?"

"Yep, they have their phones."

"Excellent! And what do you think of these, Peonies?" Julie reached in her purse and pulled out two cell phone cases, each covered with a beautiful peony flower pattern and a sprinkling of tiny rhinestones.

"Oooooh!" the girls gaped. A little piece of pizza fell out of Esme's mouth. She swallowed the rest of her bite quickly, hoping no one had noticed.

"They're gorgeous," Poppy marveled. "Did you

decorate them yourself?"

"Of course." Julie could make anything look amazing, even a plain cell phone case.

She tried passing the cases to the girls, but they both lifted their hands in the air and said simultaneously, "Pizza grease!"

"Let's sit down and eat," Sasha suggested. "Julie, grab a plate. Let's have one last dinner before we lose them to those phones."

The nine of them ate pizza and joked around the best they could. Poppy, Esme, and Will played a few rounds of UNO. Kay put on some late seventies disco. But as the evening wore on, even with presents, pizza, games, and music, the mood grew heavy.

There was a moment of excitement when Sam got a text from Milo telling him to check out his recap of the day on the East Village Update.

Pups Pop-Up Picture Parlor a Howling Success!

What a day! From 11 a.m. – 3 p.m. today in Tompkins Square Park, Esme and Poppy, the entrepreneurial girls behind PPP, popped up a puppy picture parlor, complete with props, costumes, and a painted backdrop. For four hours, a steady stream of pooches posed with or without their parents. Popeye the parrot even stopped by for a snapshot. Each $10 photo session came complete with a printed photo in a custom-made, park-themed frame which customers picked up from Lucky Stars boutique minutes *after their shoot.*

As loyal readers know, Esme and her family leave for California tomorrow, and this event was a final effort to raise enough money to buy special peony friendship necklaces.

"I was so happy to help The Peonies make this happen," Julie, proprietor of Lucky Stars, told this reporter. "And I want everyone to know. Not only did the girls make more than enough money to buy their necklaces, but they also donated what was left over to the dog run."

Wow! What a great couple of kids. And Poppy won't be the only one to miss Esme and her family. They've been in the neighborhood for over fifteen years. Best of luck in California, gang! Come back and see us sometime!

"Ugh! Maybe we should have had that going away party," Kay groaned.

Julie nodded, "Told you."

Sensing the evening was winding down, Kay, Sam, and Sasha planned the morning and gave out assignments. They'd all meet back at Sasha and Poppy's at seven fifteen. Sasha would have coffee waiting. Grady and Nico would pick up fresh bagels on the way over.

Will asked Kay, "Where's the car parked?"

"By the hardware store. I couldn't find a parking spot any closer." She rolled her eyes, dreading the idea of having to walk five blocks to get the car in the morning.

"Give me the keys," he offered. "I'll pick it up and be out front by eight to help load up and say goodbye."

Relieved, Kay tossed him the keys, and with that, Will was gone.

The boys left next, heading back to Nico's to play video games.

Then Julie took Scribbles. "No tears, Es. I'll see you soon." She gave Sam and Esme each a quick squeeze, then shared a long hug with Kay, her teacher, her mentor, and her friend.

Esme's parents left a few minutes later, holding hands as they headed out the door.

Poppy and Esme helped Sasha clean up. Then the three of them played UNO and shared memories of their beloved building and neighborhood long into the night.

Esme ran upstairs as soon as she woke up to take one last look at the only home she'd ever known. She and Kay checked cupboards, closets, and cabinets to make sure they had left nothing behind. They took everything from the fridge—sandwich meat and bread, bottled water, baby carrots, apples, and grapes—and placed it all, along with an ice pack, into their old blue cooler. Sam called the elevator and they loaded it up to take their very last trip from the sixth floor down to two.

Sasha had laid out a feast on the countertop—bagels, different flavors of whipped cream cheese, lox, capers, sliced tomatoes, and red onion. They piled up their plates, each making their own version of the perfect New York bagel. Grady and Nico quietly devoured their breakfast. Poppy and Esme just picked. They didn't even bother to put soda water in their orange juice.

The adults made small talk about which route the family would drive and the places they'd stop along the way. But the kids were all lost in their own thoughts.

Sam's phone chimed. Will was waiting outside.

"Why doesn't he come in?" Sasha asked.

"Says he's double parked. I guess we better head out there."

Everyone pitched in to carry the suitcases and the cooler out to the car in one trip—out of 2B, down in the elevator, across the lobby, and out the front door.

Esme opened the heavy metal and frosted glass door, blinking in the bright morning sun. She couldn't believe her eyes.

There was Will with the car, but also Julie and Scribbles, Liz, Chunky, and the twins, and Sir Charles, Todd, Precious, and Tab. Suzanne was there with Madeline in tow. Jimmy from Rainbow Sprinkles, Milo, Amy, and Thor. Drew, in his apron, must have slipped away from his morning baking. Mrs. Wu held frail old Mr. Wu's elbow. The sidewalk was full of friends, neighbors, their entire New York friend-family, all waiting to say goodbye.

Ms. Borden from the library handed a stack of books to Esme. "You'll need these for the car ride," she said with a warm smile. "The one on top was one of my favorites when I was your age. *Little Women* by Louisa May Alcott. It's all about sisters."

Kay and Sasha squeezed each other's hands—*Little Women* was one of their favorites, too.

Zachary stepped out from behind the group and said, "I made you a nice big jug of tea for the road." He handed it to Kay and said goodbye to each family member one by one.

"Ray's going to be in LA next month. He'll look you up," Liz stuttered, more choked up than she expected. "Don't forget to deep condition now and then, Esme."

Sam shook Mr. Wu's hand. "It's so good to see you. You didn't have to."

"Couldn't let her go without a goodbye." He looked down at Esme, whose first trip to the bodega had been in a stroller.

Mrs. Wu handed Esme a plastic container. "Your favorite."

Esme peeked under the lid at a pile of Mrs. Wu's famous sweet sesame cookies.

One by one, they said goodbye to their friends and

neighbors.

Esme managed to keep her composure until Sir Charles put his hand under her chin, looked her in the eyes, and said, “You’re a good girl, Esmeralda. I’m proud to be your friend.”

She threw her arms around his neck in a hug. “You, too.” She wanted to thank him for his patience, for everything he’d taught them over the years. But she couldn’t speak through her tears. She just hoped he knew.

The crowd finally thinned, with everyone heading off to spend their Saturdays in different ways.

The adults loaded up the car, and final hugs were exchanged all around.

Sam got behind the wheel, Grady called shotgun, and Kay slid into the backseat. Sasha, Will, and Julie stepped back into the doorway to allow Poppy and Esme a private goodbye.

The Peonies stood frozen on the sidewalk, their arms wrapped around each other.

“Text me from the road, okay?” Poppy didn’t know what else to say.

Esme nodded into her friend’s shoulder. Neither of them was ready to let go.

Finally, Sam beeped the horn and they pulled themselves apart.

“Have fun.” Poppy managed a smile.

“I’ll try.” Esme nodded.

Then Poppy held up her pinky, and the two made a final, silent pinky promise.

Esme watched out the back window as they drove away, touching her pendant, sad to leave and nervous about the future, but feeling pretty lucky to have such a great friend-family. She was happy they were leaving Poppy and Sasha surrounded by so much love.

Touching her pendant, Poppy watched Esme's face getting smaller in the window as the car got farther away. Poppy was sad to see her leave, scared about the future, but also feeling pretty lucky to have such a great friend-family. She knew that wherever Esme lived, it didn't matter. The Peonies would always be best friends.

Acknowledgements

It truly takes a village! We'd like to thank everyone who helped and encouraged us, and in particular...

Our original inspirations: Esme Marchand, Poppy Towle, Ruby Weston, and Zisa Willink.

Our earliest readers and editors: Catherine Gilbert Murdock, Drew Fitzpatrick, Elizabeth Gilbert, Julia Marchand, Julie Towle, Margaret Cordi, Rebecca Borden, and Robin Willink.

Our wonderful illustrator: Andrea Sutjipta.

Our families: Drew Fitzpatrick; Alan & Sally Sloan; John & Robin Willink; Julie, Grady, & Poppy Towle; Daimon, Julia, Milo, & Esme Marchand; Jocko, Helen, Freja, Rana, Thor, & Zisa Willink; and Douglas Sloan & Mindy Lee.

And everyone else who helped make The Peonies bloom: Aaron Smith; Amy Eyrie; Anna McClelland, Justin Merz & Genevieve Merz; Billy O'Malley; Dawn Tanner; Emily Palmquist; Erin Culley; Heather Stewart & Alex Albrecht; Jenn Krakowski; Kent Beaty & Suresh Shahi; Sandra Khawaja; Shane Eichacker; Steven Matrick; Susan Kittenplan; Suzanne Keilly & David Klotz; The Thursday Rocket Crew; and last—but certainly not least—Wendy & Ruby Weston.

And, of course, Sequoia Schmidt and the entire team at Di Angelo Publications.

About the Authors

Alix Sloan and Jennie Willink

Alix Sloan and Jennie Willink are longtime friends and creative collaborators who met in New York City and share their own lively, non-traditional friend family. Inspired by all of the amazing young people in their lives, they set out to create a story about kids like them, for kids like them—and The Peonies were born. Alix and Jennie continue to write, together and individually, and hope you enjoy the adventures of Poppy and Esme.

Visit ThePeonyChronicles.com to learn more and find links to social media.

ABOUT THE PUBLISHER

Di Angelo Publications was founded in 2008 by Sequoia Schmidt—at the age of seventeen. The modernized publishing firm's creative headquarters is in Houston, Texas, with its distribution center located in Twin Falls, Idaho. The subsidiary rights department is based in Los Angeles, and Di Angelo Publications has recently grown to include branches in England, Australia, and Sequoia's home country of New Zealand. In 2020, Di Angelo Publications made a conscious decision to move all printing and production for domestic distribution of its books to the United States. The firm is comprised of eight imprints, and the featured imprint, Emerge, was inspired by the desire to promote a love of literature, inspiration, and imagination in growing minds.

CPSIA information can be obtained
at www.ICGtesting.com
Printed in the USA
BVHW042134060622
639095BV00004B/105